A FIRST TREASURY *of* NURSERY STORIES

For Clara Sutherland – M.H.
For Olivia, with love – A.C.

A FIRST TREASURY *of* NURSERY STORIES

Retold by
MARY HOFFMAN

Illustrated by
ANNA CURREY

First published in 2000 by Macmillan Children's Books,
a division of Macmillan Publishers Limited,
25 Eccleston Place, London SW1W 9NF,
Basingstoke and Oxford,
www.macmillan.com
Associated companies around the world.

ISBN 0 333 76579 6

A CIP catalogue record for this book is available from the British Library.

Colour reproduction by Speedscan Ltd

Printed and bound in Great Britain by Bath Press

Contents

Oh, Grandma, What Big Ears You Have

Animal Stories

You Shall Go to the Ball

Stories About Transformations

 You Can't Catch Me,
I'm the Gingerbread Man

Nonsense Stories

Turn Again, Whittington

Resourceful Heroes and Heroines

 Slow and Steady Wins the Race

Stories with a Moral

Mirror, Mirror, on the Wall

Magical Stories

 Fee, Fi, Fo, Fum

Quick Wits and Giantkilling

Introduction

"Treasury" is a word we use so often that we have almost stopped noticing that it is a metaphor. But a treasury is more than just a collection. It acknowledges the priceless value of each item, its diversity, desirability and beauty.

That is exactly how I feel about the stories in this volume. They spill out of the gorgeous container Anna Currey has crafted for them, full of colour, sparkle and sheen. Some are stately in their loveliness, like "East o' the Sun and West o' the Moon" or "The Six Swans". Some are great vulgar bits of costume jewellery, like "Clever Gretel" or "The Three Wishes".

All I have done is to untangle them and polish them up a bit so that they can be seen to best advantage, particularly the pieces which have been languishing in the attics of memory for rather a long time.

Although I'm not in favour of bowdlerising fairy tales, when I read over the sources for some of the stories here I did find some of the scenes, particularly the endings, to be unnecessarily cruel and violent. Retribution is all very well, but punishments involving beheadings or boiling wolves alive belong to an older order where revenge, rather than mercy, was the dominant mood. So I have taken the liberty, for the young readership of this book, of toning down some of the endings. You can find the original endings in the sources listed.

It's hard for me to imagine growing up without these stories, but one of the reasons for compiling another treasury is that there is some evidence that children and, even more sadly, their parents and teachers, don't seem to know these basic stories any more.

I was a very lucky little girl. My family had very little money, but what I did have was parents and a big sister who read to me, a well-stocked library within walking distance and a primary school where story-telling was taken for granted.

Our headmaster used to tell us stories in assembly—I'm sure that's where I first heard "The Sun and the Wind"—and our class teachers read to us all the time, at least that's how I remember it. Thank you, Honeywell Primary!

Another powerful influence on my childhood was the radio. I realise that many of the retellings here, such as "The Three Billy Goats Gruff", "The Little Red Hen" and "The Gingerbread Man" come straight from my memory of listening to a programme called "Children's Favourites" on the BBC's old Home Service.

So, most of what you will find in this book has been a part of my world for half a century. I can't imagine life without knowing about Cinderella's pumpkin-coach, Little Red Riding-Hood's encounter with the wolf, the princess who could feel a pea under twenty mattresses and so on. But some stories came to me in later life, as when my mother-in-law told my daughters "The Three Heads in the Well" and I read "Brave Molly Whuppie" and "Kate Crackernuts" as an adult. That is how it should be, adding new stories to our mental repertoire all the time.

My all time favourite when I was small was Hans Andersen's "The Little Mermaid". I am very happy to include it here, restoring its original sad ending. The poignancy of the mermaid's

hopeless love for the prince who didn't even know of her sacrifice was an important part of why I loved the story so much. Disney did children a disservice in fudging up a spurious happy ending, which doesn't accord with those moving and memorable images about walking on knives.

If a story doesn't have to be jolly to mean a lot to a child, what qualities does it have to have? The important thing is that it teaches us something about our humanity. Motifs recur, some touching on qualities which adults may want to suppress in children: disobedience, risk-taking, jealousy, greed. Others are of self-denial, loving sacrifice, loyalty, bravery.

Virtue is rewarded and the villains get their come-uppance. Although I have sometimes toned down these final punishments, though I have left the fates of one or two unfortunate wolves, by and large I have not changed the essentials of these stories. They teach us a lot but they would not have survived if they did not also entertain.

I hope this book will help to entertain a whole new generation and give them something to treasure.

Mary Hoffman, 2000

Oh, Grandma,

What Big Ears You Have

Animal Stories

The Three Little Pigs

There was once an old mother pig who had three piglets. Food was short in their home so, as soon as the three little pigs were old enough, they packed some lunch into their red spotted handkerchiefs and set off to seek their fortune.

The three pigs walked down the road together and met a man carrying a load of straw.

"This is my chance," said the first little pig. "Please give me that straw and I shall build myself a house."

The man gave the pig his straw and the pig built

himself a cosy little house of straw, while his brothers went on their way, still seeking their fortune.

No sooner had the first pig settled himself snugly in his straw house than along came the big bad wolf. He peered through the tiny gap in the straw that the pig had left for a window and saw the chance of a nice dinner for himself.

"Little pig, little pig, let me come in," said the wolf.

"No, no, not by the hairs on my chinny-chin-chin," squeaked the terrified pig. "I'll not let you in."

"Then I'll huff and I'll puff and I'll BLOW YOUR HOUSE DOWN!" said the wolf, and he was as good as his word.

He huffed and he puffed and he blew the straw house right down and gobbled the little pig all up.

As the two other little pigs walked along the road, they met a man carrying a large bundle of twigs.

"Aha," said the second little pig. "This is where I get my chance. Please give me those twigs and I shall build myself a house."

And the man gave him the twigs, while the third little pig carried on seeking his fortune.

The second pig built a house of twigs, which were much stronger than straw. But as soon as he was inside it, there was the eye of the big bad wolf peeping through a space between two twigs and spying on him.

"Little pig, little pig, let me come in," he said.

"No, no, not by the hairs on my chinny-chin-chin," squealed the pig. "I'll not let you in."

"Then I'll huff and I'll puff and I'll BLOW YOUR HOUSE DOWN!" said the wolf, and he was as good as his word.

He huffed and he puffed and he blew the twig house right down and gobbled the little pig all up.

The third pig walked cheerfully along the road, all by himself, until he met a man pushing a barrow full of bricks.

"Please will you give me those bricks, so that I can build a house for myself?" asked the little pig, and the man handed them over.

The pig built himself a really strong house out of bricks, with proper windows and a door and even a chimney. He sat down by his fire and then saw something outside his window. It was the big bad wolf.

"Little pig, little pig, let me come in," said the wolf.

"No, no, not by the hairs on my chinny-chin-chin," said the pig calmly. "I'll not let you in."

"Then I'll huff and I'll puff and I'll BLOW YOUR HOUSE DOWN!" said the wolf.

So the wolf huffed and he puffed. And he puffed and he huffed.

But he could not blow the brick house down.

The wolf was exhausted. And he was also furious. He was determined to eat that little pig.

So the next day he came back and said, "Little pig, I know where there is a good field of turnips."

"Where?" asked the pig.

"In Farmer Smith's field," said the wolf. "I'll take you there at six o'clock tomorrow morning."

The pig agreed but next morning he got up at five o'clock and went to Farmer Smith's field and fetched himself a nice load of turnips and was back in his house before the wolf arrived.

The wolf was very cross to have been tricked.

"Little pig," he said. "I know where there is a fine tree full of apples."

"Where?" asked the pig.

"At Merrydown," said the wolf, "and if you promise not to trick me, I'll take you there at five o'clock tomorrow morning."

The little pig agreed but next day he got up at four o'clock and went to Merrydown and climbed the apple tree. But it was further away than the turnip field and he was still up the tree when the wolf came loping along.

"What?" said the wolf. "Here before me? Are the apples nice?"

"Very nice," said the pig. "Would you like one?"

He threw an apple quite a long way from the tree and while the wolf was fetching it, the little pig ran down and back to his brick house and shut himself safely indoors.

As soon as he realised he had been tricked again, the wolf raced back to the house of bricks.

"There's a fair," he panted, "this afternoon at Shanklin. I'll come for you at three o'clock if you like."

The pig agreed but at two o'clock he made his own way to the fair. He was having a lovely time eating

toffee apples and candyfloss when he suddenly saw the wolf. Quickly, he climbed into an empty barrel and rolled down the hill towards the wolf.

The wolf was terrified as the barrel rolled faster and

faster. He jumped out of the way and the barrel rolled to the bottom of the hill where the little pig's house was. The pig ran into his house and soon heard the wolf gasping outside.

"Oh dear, what a fright I've had! I went to the fair and a great big round thing rolled down the hill after me and I had to jump out of its way to save my life!"

"Ha!" said the little pig. "That was me inside a barrel!"

The wolf was so angry that he was determined to get the little pig somehow. He started to climb onto the roof. But the little pig guessed what he was up to and put a great big saucepan of water to boil on his fire.

So when the wolf finally managed to squeeze down the chimney, he fell plop into a pan of boiling water! How he howled! The wolf ran out of the little pig's brick house, clutching his burnt bottom . . . and was never seen again.

The Musicians of Bremen

There was once a donkey who had worked all his life for a miller but was now getting old. He knew that the miller couldn't afford to keep him as a pet so he decided to set out for the town of Bremen and become a musician there. After all, he could sing a fine "hee-haw!"

On his way he met a dog, lying by the side of the road and panting. "What's the matter?" asked the donkey.

"I've run away from home," said the dog. "I am too old to hunt any more and I think my master was planning to shoot me."

"Then why not come with me?" said the donkey. "I'm going to Bremen to be a musician. You could do that, too. You know how to howl, I suppose?"

When the dog had recovered, the two new friends walked on towards Bremen. After a short while they came across a cat sitting on the path looking very sorry for itself.

"What's the matter?" they asked.

"My teeth are not as sharp as they were and I've lost the taste for catching mice, so my mistress has thrown me out."

"Then come with us to Bremen," said the donkey and the dog. "We are going to be musicians and you could join us. We know how tunefully cats sing at night."

Not long after this the three companions passed a farm and there sat a cock on the gatepost, crowing with all his might.

"It's not morning," said the other animals. "Why are you crowing now?"

"I heard my mistress say I was getting too old. I am supposed to be turned into stew tomorrow, so I'm singing as much as I can today."

"Well, bring your fine singing voice to Bremen with us," said the others. "Wouldn't you rather be a musician than end up in the pot?"

The cock agreed and the four friends went on their way. When night fell, they settled in a wood. The donkey and the dog lay at the foot of a tree, while the cat climbed up into its branches and the cock flew right to the top.

While he was up there, the cock saw a distant light. He flew down to tell his friends.

"I think there's a house over there. Perhaps we could find better lodging and maybe some food?"

So they set off towards the light. It came from a very cosy house on the edge of the wood. The donkey, being the tallest, looked in at the window and came back to tell them what he had seen.

"It's a robbers' house," he said. "They are all sitting round a table and it is absolutely loaded with good things to eat and drink."

So the four friends made a plan. The donkey went back to the window and the dog climbed up on his back and the cat sat on the dog's shoulders, while the cock perched on the cat's head. Then they gave their first concert.

The donkey hee-hawed, the dog howled, the cat

caterwauled and the cock crowed "cock-a-doodle-doo!" They all burst through the window at the same time and the robbers were so terrified of the noise, thinking it must be a ghost, that they ran away into the woods.

The four friends had a very good meal of the robbers' food and then settled down to sleep in the places that suited them best. The donkey lay on some straw in the yard. The dog slept behind the door, the cat curled up near the remains of the fire and the cock flew up into the rafters.

The robbers began to get over their fright and sent one member of the gang back to the house to see what was going on. In he crept, but the house was in darkness now, so he thought he would light a taper at the fire. He mistook the cat's eyes for two burning coals and poked the taper at them.

The cat shrieked and flew at the man's face, scratching him with her claws. He stumbled over the dog by the door, who bit him in the leg. He ran out into the yard, where the donkey kicked him hard and the cock flew down from the rafters crowing "cock-a-doodle-doo!"

The robber got back to his friends in a terrible state.

"There's a dreadful witch in the house," he cried. "She scratched me and cursed me. And then a man with a knife stabbed me in the leg as I was coming out of the door and a monster was waiting in the yard, who beat me with a wooden club! And then a judge called from up on the roof—'There's nothing you can do!'—so I ran away as fast as I could."

When his companions saw the robber's scratches and bruises, no one dared go back to the house. So the four friends lived there in happiness to the end of their days and never reached Bremen at all.

The Ugly Duckling

It was lovely warm sunny weather when the mother duck laid her eggs in a quiet place by the river. She got very bored with sitting on them, waiting for them to hatch, because she missed her friends in the farmyard.

But at last the eggshells began to crack and the little ducklings poked their heads out. "Oh, what sweet babies!" cried the duck, counting her young. "One, two, three, four, five . . . oh bother! Number six has still not hatched."

The sixth egg was much bigger than all the others and, to tell the truth, the mother duck wasn't sure that it was one of hers. Birds can be very absent-minded about that sort of thing. Still, she sat on it for a few more days and at last it, too, began to crack. And out came the ugliest duckling she had ever seen.

He was much bigger than his pretty little brothers and sisters and had dull grey feathers, while theirs were fluffy yellow and brown.

"Oh dear," thought the mother duck. "Perhaps he's a turkey?"

But the ugly duckling could swim just as well as the others. His mother led them all back down the river to the duck pond in the farmyard.

"Look, here comes another clutch of ducklings," said one of the older ducks. "As if we didn't have enough mouths to feed."

"And look at that one!" said another. "That's the ugliest duckling I've ever seen!" One by one all the ducks in the farmyard noticed the new duckling. And all the hens noticed him. And all the turkeys. And they all said how ugly he was. The poor duckling felt very lonely. The girl who fed the birds was mean to him and tried to kick him. And even his own brothers and sisters teased him and called him names.

So the ugly duckling swam away from the farm along the river and found his own pond. He had no one to talk to, but one day he saw a flock of beautiful white birds flying in the sky. He didn't know what they were but his heart yearned towards them.

"Oh, how lovely to fly free with those beautiful birds," he thought. And he felt very sorry for himself. But he soon felt sorrier, when the warm days of summer were followed by the frosts of autumn and the freezing snow of winter. He had to swim round and round in circles in his pond to stop it from icing over. There was very little to eat and the ugly duckling had a wretched time of it.

Finally the spring came. The flowers started to bloom and fill the air with their scent, and the ugly duckling felt hopeful again. His wings were big and strong now and he started to fly. He flew and flew until he came to a beautiful garden full of flowers with a stream running through it.

The ugly duckling landed in the water and then around the corner came three of the beautiful white birds he had seen the year before.

"I will join them," thought the ugly duckling, "though I'm sure they will jeer at me like all the other birds."

But they didn't. They were three swans and they greeted the ugly duckling like a long-lost brother. He was so shy he lowered his head — and then he saw his own reflection in the water. He wasn't a duck at all — he was a swan!

Some children in the garden saw him and called out, "Look, there's a new swan! And he's much the handsomest."

They threw bread and cake crumbs into the water and made sure the new swan got plenty. The bird who used to be an ugly duckling was so happy. He had gone from being teased and bullied to being the handsomest swan in the garden. He spread his lovely white wings and stretched his lovely white neck and then he hid his head under his wing. He couldn't believe how lucky he was.

Little Red Riding-Hood

There was once a pretty little girl who lived with her mother and father in a country village. Her father was a woodcutter and both her parents and her grandmother loved her better than anything in the world. Her grandmother made her a red cape with a hood such as fine ladies of those days wore when they went riding.

The little girl loved her red cape and wore it so often that everyone called her Little Red Riding-Hood, though her name was Biddy. One day, her mother said to Little Red Riding-Hood, "I want you to visit your grandmother. She hasn't been well so I have made her a dish of custard. Here, it's in this basket with a little butter and some other goodies."

It was a lovely day and Little Red Riding-Hood was happy to go. Her grandmother lived in the next village and she had to walk through a wood but she wasn't afraid. She could hear her father and some other men cutting down trees in the wood. Little Red Riding-Hood sang as she went and would have skipped but she was worried about spilling the custard.

As she walked carefully along the path, all of a sudden a big hairy wolf stepped out in front of her. He would have eaten her up straight away, but he knew the woodcutters were nearby. So he just said, "Where are you going, little girl?"

"To see my grandmother, who isn't well," answered Little Red Riding-Hood. "I am taking her a custard."

"And where does your grandmother live?" asked the wolf, thinking he might get two meals in one.

"It's the first house in the next village," said Little Red Riding-Hood, who was a polite little girl.

So the wolf ran ahead and reached the grandmother's cottage first. He knocked at the door — tock, tock.

"Who's there?" called the grandmother.

The wolf tried to sound like a little girl. "It's me, Granny," he squeaked. "Mummy has sent me with a custard."

The grandmother didn't feel well enough to get up. "Just lift the latch and let yourself in, dear," she said.

So the wolf lifted the latch and bounded into the cottage. He grabbed Little Red Riding-Hood's grandmother and gobbled her up in one big bite.

Meanwhile, Little Red Riding-Hood reached the cottage and knocked at the door — tock, tock.

"Who is it?" came a gruff voice.

"Grandma must have a very bad sore throat," thought the little girl. "It's me, Little Red Riding-Hood," she called out loud.

"Just lift the latch and let yourself in, dear," said the voice.

So Little Red Riding-Hood lifted the latch and let herself in. The curtains were drawn and it was dark inside the cottage but, as the little girl approached the bed, she didn't think her grandmother looked quite right.

"Come closer and give your old Granny a kiss," said the wolf. You see, the wolf had put the grandmother's nightie and bonnet on and had hidden under the bedclothes! Little Red Riding-Hood went closer.

"Oh, Grandma, what big ears you have," she said, looking at the wolf's furry ears.

"All the better to hear you with, my dear," said the wolf.

"Oh, Grandma, what big eyes you have," said Little Red Riding-Hood, seeing the wolf's eyes glittering in the dark.

"All the better to see you with, my dear," said the wolf.

"Oh, Grandma, what big teeth you have," shrieked Little Red Riding-Hood as she looked at the wolf's terrible mouth.

"All the better to EAT you with, my dear!" snarled the wolf and he leapt out of bed and swallowed Little Red Riding-Hood on the spot.

But on the way down his throat she screamed for help so loudly that the woodcutters heard her.

They came rushing to the cottage and the first one, who happened to be Little Red Riding-Hood's father, split the wolf's stomach with his axe. Out came Little Red Riding-Hood. Out came the grandmother. They were not much the worse for wear and they all celebrated their lucky escape.

But the wolf was dead, of course.

The Country Mouse
and the
City Mouse

There were once two mice who were good friends. One was a house mouse who lived in a big city and the other was a field mouse who lived in the countryside.

The city mouse paid his friend a visit in the country and the field mouse was very glad to see him.

"Come with me and we will have a feast of ripe barley

and wheat," he said.

The city mouse ate a good dinner but he didn't seem satisfied.

"Ah," he sighed. "You should see what I get to eat in the town — cheese, figs, honey, sultanas, apples. You would soon tire of all this field-food if you tasted city life. Why don't you come and stay with me so I can show you?"

So the country mouse went home with his friend. He was very frightened by all the many pairs of feet and carriage wheels on the street and very relieved when they reached the city mouse's house.

As soon as the city mouse had shown his friend his comfortable home behind the skirting board, they set out to find their dinner.

"You see how conveniently my home is situated,"

boasted the city mouse. "In the kitchen, the best room in all the house."

He led his friend through a tiny crack at the bottom of a door into a larder, where there were the most delicious smells. The little country mouse's mouth watered. They scampered up onto a high shelf where there sat a tasty cheese. But no sooner had they started to nibble the edges off it than a large person opened the larder door and reached for the shelf!

The mice scuttled away and hid. When all was quiet again they came out and this time climbed onto the kitchen table. In the middle of it was a handsome cake, made with sultanas and cherries and many other kinds of dried fruit. The country mouse's whiskers twitched. This was finer fare than he ever found in a field.

But they had not tasted more than a crumb of the cake's icing before someone else came into the room and they had to run and hide again. Back in the city mouse's hole, the country mouse gasped for breath, his little heart pounding.

"You can keep your fine city food," he panted. "I grant you it is very fine indeed and probably delicious but you have to put up with so many dangers to get it that, as for me, I would rather eat the humble grains I find in the fields than risk so much to get fancier meals."

And he headed back to the country where he lived happily for the rest of his days, though he never tasted cake. And the city mouse lived happily, too, because he was used to the dangers of his way of life and much too fond of cake to leave it behind.

Goldilocks and
the Three Bears

Once upon a time there were three bears who lived together in a pretty cottage in the middle of a forest. One was a Great Huge Bear with a deep gruff voice, another was a Middle-Sized Bear with a low tuneful voice and the third was a Small Wee Bear with a high squeaky voice. They each had a bed, a chair and a porridge-bowl of exactly the right size to suit each one of them.

One day, after they had made their breakfast porridge, they went for a walk in the forest, to let it cool down so that it would not burn their mouths. And while they were away, a little girl called Goldilocks came tripping up the path to their front door.

She had been walking in the forest without telling her parents, which was very naughty. She had lost her way chasing butterflies and one particularly handsome red and yellow one had led her to the bears' house. Of course she didn't know it belonged to three bears, but by then she was very hungry, so she knocked on the door. There was no answer, so she lifted the latch and stepped inside.

Goldilocks found herself in the nicest kitchen, with a stone floor, a big iron cooking range and a comfortable tabby cat sleeping on a rag rug. On the scrubbed wooden table, Goldilocks found three bowls of porridge, with three spoons beside them. She couldn't help herself; she hadn't had any breakfast. She dipped a spoon into the biggest bowl and took a taste.

"Oh!" cried Goldilocks, "I can't eat that—it's much too hot."

Then she tried the porridge in the middle-sized bowl.

"Ugh!" cried Goldilocks, "I can't eat that—it's much too cold!"

Then she tried the smallest bowl.

"Yum, yum!" said Goldilocks. "Not too hot and not too cold. It's just right!"

And she ate it all up.

In the kitchen were three armchairs. Goldilocks went and sat in the biggest one.

"I don't like this chair," she said, wriggling her bottom. "It's much too hard."

So she tried the middle-sized chair.

"I don't like this one either," said Goldilocks. "It's much too soft."

So she jumped off that one, too. And then she sat in the smallest chair. "Aah!" sighed Goldilocks. "Not too hard

and not too soft. It's just right." And she
snuggled so hard into the smallest
chair that it broke in pieces!

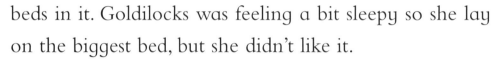

"Oops!" said Goldilocks
and decided to explore
upstairs. She found a
cosy bedroom with three
beds in it. Goldilocks was feeling a bit sleepy so she lay
on the biggest bed, but she didn't like it.

"The blankets are much too heavy," said Goldilocks
and she climbed into the middle-sized bed.

"The covers are much too light," she complained and
put herself into the smallest bed.

"Lovely!" said Goldilocks. "This duvet is not too heavy
and not too light. It's just right."

And she curled up all cosily in the
smallest bed and fell fast asleep.

Now, the three bears who
lived in the little cottage were
coming back from their walk.
As soon as they got into their
kitchen, the Great Huge Bear
looked at his bowl and

growled in his deep gruff voice, "Who's been eating my porridge?"

The Middle-Sized Bear looked at her bowl and sighed in her low tuneful voice, "Who's been eating my porridge?"

And the Small Wee Bear took one look at his bowl and squeaked in his little high voice, "Who's been eating my porridge?—and has eaten it all up!"

The Great Huge Bear sat down. "Who's been sitting in my chair?" he growled in his deep gruff voice.

The Middle-Sized Bear sat down. "Who's been sitting in my chair?" she sighed in her low tuneful voice.

And the Small Wee Bear couldn't sit down at all. "Who's been sitting in my chair?" he squeaked in his little high voice, "and has broken it all in pieces!"

The three bears went upstairs. The Great Huge Bear looked at his bed. "Who's been sleeping in my bed?" he growled in his deep gruff voice.

The Middle-Sized Bear looked at her bed. "Who's been sleeping in my bed?" she

sighed in her low tuneful voice.

And the Small Wee Bear looked at his bed and squeaked in his little high voice, "Who's been sleeping in my bed? And is *still* sleeping in my bed? There's a little girl in my bed!"

In her sleep Goldilocks heard the Great Huge Bear's voice like the sound of a deep buzz saw in the forest, then the Middle-Sized Bear's voice like leaves sighing in an autumn wind and then the Small Wee Bear's voice like the high-pitched squeaking of a family of mice. And when she heard the high-pitched squeaking, she sat bolt upright in the bed.

And what should she see but three furry brown bears looking down at her! She sprang out of bed and ran towards the open window. Goldilocks was so afraid of the bears though, to tell the truth, they were very mild and gentle ones, that she jumped right out of the window. Luckily it wasn't a long drop, so she was able to run off home.

The bears scratched their heads and went back downstairs to make a fresh pot of porridge. They never found out who Goldilocks was and they never saw her again.

The Wolf and
the Seven Little Kids

There was once a nanny goat who had seven little kids, whom she loved as dearly as any human mother ever loved her babies. One day she had to go into the forest to fetch some food, but she was worried about a wolf who lived nearby. So she called all her seven children to her and gave them some advice.

"My dear little kids, I must go and get us some food. Now while I am away, you must watch out for the wolf.

He is very good at disguises, but you should know him by his rough voice and his black feet."

"Don't worry, Mother," said the kids. "We will take care of one another."

So away she went. Not long afterwards someone came to the door and knocked, saying, "Let me in, dear little kids. It is your mother come back and I have something nice for each of you to eat."

But it was a harsh rough voice and the little kids bleated, "You are not our mother! She has a soft gentle voice and yours is so horrid you must be the wolf!"

The wolf went to a shop and bought himself a huge pot of honey. He ate the lot and it made his voice soft and pleasant. Then he went back to the goats' house and knocked on the door, saying, "Dear little kids, let me in. It is I, your mother, and I have something nice for each of you to eat."

But while he was talking, the wolf laid his black paws against the window and the kids cried out, "You are not our mother! She has sweet white woolly feet. Yours are so hairy and black, you must be the wolf!"

Cursing and growling, the wolf ran to the mill and told

the miller to sprinkle his paws with white flour. At first the miller said no, guessing the wolf was trying to deceive someone. But the wolf threatened to eat him if he didn't, so the miller sprinkled the wolf's paws with flour.

A third time the wolf came to the goats' house and called, "Dear little kids, let me in. It is I, your mother, and I have something nice for each of you to eat."

"Show us your feet," said the kids.

And the wolf obligingly put his floury paws on the window sill. The kids were quite convinced it was their mother this time and opened the door. Whoosh! In rushed the wolf, and the kids all scattered. One hid under the table, one in the bed, one inside the stove, one in a cupboard, one behind the woodpile and one inside the washing bowl. The seventh and youngest little kid hid inside the case of the grandfather clock.

The wolf found them all except the seventh and ate them all up.

Not long afterwards the nanny goat came home. How upset she was to see the door open, the table knocked on its side and the washing bowl broken on the floor. She ran about the house distracted with worry, calling her kids by name. But it wasn't until she called the seventh one that she heard any reply. "Is that you, Mother?" called the frightened little kid from inside the grandfather clock.

How she embraced her one remaining child, weeping as she heard what had happened to the other six. In her grief she wandered out of the house, with the last little kid trotting behind her, and strayed into a nearby meadow.

There they found the wolf sleeping off his huge meal. The poor goat saw something squirming in his stomach and thought, "Could it be that my children are still alive?" She sent the littlest kid back to the house to fetch a knife and a needle and strong thread. When he got back, the goat cut open the wolf's stomach. He had been so greedy that he had swallowed the six little kids whole! One by one they came popping out of the cut that their mother had made.

What rejoicing there was when the mother and her precious children were

reunited! The wolf slept on and while he snored, the kids found some big stones and put them in his stomach and the goat sewed him up again with the needle and thread. Then the goat and the seven little kids went and hid behind a tree to see what would happen.

When the wolf woke up he felt terribly thirsty but, as he walked towards the stream to quench his thirst, the stones in his stomach knocked together and made him feel very peculiar.

When he reached the stream, the wolf put his head down to drink and the weight of the stones unbalanced him so that he fell into the water and drowned.

As soon as the seven little kids saw what had happened to the wolf, they danced for joy, singing:

> "The wolf is gone, the wolf is drowned,
> The kids he ate have all been found.
> The wolf is drowned, the wolf is dead
> We'll eat our supper and go to bed!"

You Shall Go to the Ball

Stories About
Transformations

Beauty and the Beast

There was once a rich merchant who had six children:
three sons and three daughters. He happily spent his
money on their education and they all had fine clothes
and valuable ornaments and jewellery. They were all
good-looking young people, but the youngest daughter
was the most attractive of all of them. When she was small,
she was known as "the little beauty" and the name stuck.
She had no name but Beauty.

This did not make her popular with her two sisters,
who were not very nice-natured. They were jealous of

Beauty, who was as kind and sweet as she was pretty. The older sisters were very vain and proud and wouldn't have anything to do with the other merchants' daughters.

They were often courted by young men, since they were handsome, but they always said, "Oh, no, we wouldn't marry anyone lower than a Duke!" Beauty had her admirers, too, but she just said, "Thank you, but I am too young to marry. I want to stay with my father a few years more."

Then disaster struck. The merchant's ships were all lost at sea, with all his goods upon them. He had to sell his fine house in town and his carriage and retire to a small farm he owned in the country. The merchant and his sons now worked long hours on their land and there was no money for luxuries.

It took Beauty a few weeks to adjust to her new life. She didn't miss the balls and the dancing and the fine dresses, but it was hard to get up at four every morning and light the fires and cook the food for the family. But Beauty did all this and grew strong, while her sisters stayed in bed till ten o'clock and spent the whole day lamenting their loss of fortune.

Then, one day, a message reached the merchant that one of his ships had survived and was coming into a nearby port. The old man's heart leapt to think that he might recover some of his money and perhaps relieve Beauty of some of her household burdens. His two oldest daughters thought only of regaining their finery and asked him to bring back ever so many trinkets and fripperies from the town.

"What about you, Beauty?" asked her father. "Is there nothing you would like?"

Beauty thought hard, because she didn't want her father to spend any of his regained money on frivolities. "I should like a rose, Father," she said at last, thinking she was asking for something simple and little knowing how much trouble it would cause.

Well, the merchant rode to the port and his ship had indeed returned, but his debts were so great that he had to sell everything on board it to pay for them. There was nothing left over for even a scrap of lace for a flighty daughter. He was a bitter man as he rode back home after his wasted journey.

But his problems increased as the weather worsened. First, the rain came down and then there was thunder and lightning. The merchant's clothes were drenched and his horse was a sorry sight. They were in the middle of a wild wood, lashed by wind and rain.

Just when he thought he couldn't bear any more discomfort, the merchant saw a light through the trees. He urged his horse towards it, and found a splendid castle, all illuminated but with no sign of life in it.

The horse found his way to a stable and tucked in

eagerly to the hay and oats he found there. The merchant rubbed him down with some straw and tied him to the manger.

Then he entered the castle itself, calling out as he went but seeing no one. The merchant's wet footsteps squelched on the thick carpets as he made his way from room to room.

He found a dining-room, with a table laid for one, and went over to the roaring fire in the grate. He was soon warm and reasonably dry, but very hungry.

At last, at about eleven o'clock, the merchant could bear it no longer. He ate the cold roast chicken and drank a glass or two of wine. Then he felt very sleepy and wandered off to find a bedroom. No sooner did he spy a comfortable-looking bed, than he fell on it and into a deep sleep.

When he woke, refreshed, the next morning, the merchant was astonished to find his weather-stained clothes removed and a new suit in his size laid out for him. "This castle must belong to a kind fairy!" he exclaimed. He went hopefully back to the dining-room and found hot chocolate and a good breakfast waiting for him.

"Thank you, kind fairy," he said, as he went out to the stable to collect his horse. He was leading him out through the gardens, when he noticed a splendid rose-bush and remembered Beauty. "I may not have anything for my other daughters," he thought, "but I could at least take Beauty her rose." And he broke a branch off the bush.

All of a sudden, there was a terrifying growling and a monstrous beast came through the garden.

"Ungrateful wretch!" he roared. "I have fed you and housed you and given you fresh garments and this is how you repay me, by stealing my roses, which are more precious to me than anything else. For this you will die!"

And the beast made as if to devour the merchant on the spot. The poor man fell to his knees and begged for mercy. "Forgive me, my lord. I had no idea they meant so much to you. I was only going to take some roses for my youngest daughter, Beauty."

"Talk not to me of daughters!" growled the beast. "Nor call me 'my lord'. My name is Beast, and I tell you, I shall eat you for your impertinence. But I am willing to wait three months. Give me your word that you will return here then, if one of your children does not volunteer to take your place."

"I promise, my . . . Beast," said the merchant, thinking that at least he would see his children again before he died. Then the Beast seemed to relent a bit. "Before you go," he said, "you may return to your room and put in a chest that you will find there anything you want to take. It will be sent on to you. I am not an ungenerous host; I just can't bear people taking my roses."

So the merchant went back and packed the chest with large gold pieces that he found in his room. He wept as he did so, thinking that he would be able to lighten his children's poverty, though at a terrible cost.

He travelled home with a heavy heart, but took comfort from the welcome his children gave him, especially Beauty. He gave her the branch of roses, but could not help saying as he did so, "Here are your roses, but I am likely to pay for them with my life."

Then his children wouldn't rest till they had got the whole story out of him. "Huh!" said his oldest daughter. "Typical of Beauty!"

"Yes," said the other. "Look how she doesn't even shed a tear for her father's life!"

"That is because I know he will not have to give it," said Beauty, calmly. "It was my fault that the Beast was enraged, so I shall go in my father's place."

Her brothers said they couldn't allow it, that they would go with weapons and kill the Beast, but Beauty said she would not dream of endangering their lives. Her father said he had only a few years left to live and it was better for him to die than one so young and lovely with her life before her. But Beauty was not persuaded. She told her father that he could not stop her from accompanying him in three months' time. Her sisters didn't attempt to dissuade her at all; they were quite pleased at the idea of getting rid of her.

The next morning, the merchant was amazed to find the chest of gold pieces by his bed. He told no one about it but Beauty, who said, "Father, while you were away, two suitors came asking for my sisters in marriage. Do use some of this money for their dowries."

"I believe you are right, Beauty. It would give me great comfort to know that they were settled in life, before I keep my promise to the Beast," said the merchant, who could still not accept that Beauty was going to stand in for him.

But when it was time for him to return to the Beast's castle, Beauty saddled her own little pony and rode beside him. Her sisters had to rub their eyes with an onion to feign tears, but her brothers were genuinely sad to see her go.

When they arrived at the castle, the horses took themselves to the stable and the merchant led Beauty to the dining-room. There were two places laid and the merchant, knowing a little more of how the castle worked this time, urged Beauty to sit and eat. Neither of them had much of an appetite.

After supper, they heard the growling noise which meant that the Beast was approaching. Brave as she was, Beauty's heart quaked within her. And when she saw him, she was almost faint with terror. But the Beast was very courteous and polite. Even at the last minute, Beauty's father tried to persuade her to change her mind, but she was quite resolute.

She said goodbye to her father with many tears and the Beast withdrew. Alone in the castle, Beauty found a door with "BEAUTY'S CHAMBER" written above it. Inside was a beautiful room, all fitted out with the finest silks and satins and a large four-poster bed. There were books to read and painting materials and a harpsichord.

"Would the Beast really have gone to so much trouble if he meant to eat me straightaway?" thought Beauty. She went to bed and, in spite of her situation, slept well.

In the morning, servants brought her gorgeous dresses to choose from, all made specially to her size and, again, Beauty thought that this would not have been done if she were to die soon. She passed a pleasant day in her comfortable room and wandering through the castle's beautiful gardens.

At supper time, she heard the Beast coming and had to screw up all her courage to face him. But he merely asked if he might sit with her while she ate, and she could hardly object.

"Do you find me very ugly?" asked the Beast, and Beauty found it difficult to answer. She didn't want to hurt his feelings.

"Perhaps you are somewhat ugly in appearance," she said, "but you seem to be kind and you have exquisite manners."

The Beast was pleased with her answer. And so a pattern developed to their days. Beauty played her harpsichord and painted pictures and read books and went for long walks. Anything she wanted appeared magically before her. Indeed, when she wished to know how her father was, the looking-glass in her room immediately showed her a picture of him returning home.

Over the weeks, she saw in the mirror that her sisters were married and that her father and brothers were still sad about her absence. She had no more fears about being eaten by the Beast. She saw him only at supper time, but came to look forward to his visits. It was the only company she had and she enjoyed their conversations.

The only thing that troubled her was that the Beast asked her to marry him. She said no, but he repeated his request every evening. It distressed her to upset him, but she said, "Dear Beast, you know I am very fond of you and I know you have a kind heart and a good nature. But I can never marry you."

One night, when he had received his answer, the Beast said, "If you will not marry me, Beauty, promise me this —that you will never leave me."

Beauty thought about it. She was really happy at the castle and wanted for nothing and she had become really very used to the Beast and fond of him.

"I will promise you that," said Beauty, "if you will let me have one visit home first to see my father and family again."

"I can deny you nothing," said the Beast, "but you must return after a week, or I shall die of grief. Just place this ring on your bedside table when you want to return."

Next morning, when Beauty awoke, she found to her delight that she was in her father's house. How the maid screamed when she entered the room to clean it! Beauty's father and brothers were overjoyed to see her. They sent for her sisters, who came with their husbands. But Beauty was sad to see that they were not as happy and contented as she was.

The first one had married a very handsome man, but he was so vain and selfish that he didn't really care about anyone but himself. The second had married a very agreeable and witty man but, after their marriage, he used his wit at her expense and was very sarcastic and cruel.

The sisters were green with jealousy to see Beauty's fine clothes and to observe how well she looked and to hear how happy she was with the Beast. Secretly, they plotted to keep her longer than a week. "Perhaps then he will be angry and come and eat her after all," they said.

So, when the week was up, they pretended they couldn't do without Beauty and persuaded her to stay a few days. She was worried about the Beast, but didn't like to upset her sisters, who were not usually so nice to her.

But, after a few days, she had a terrible dream. The Beast was lying in his rose garden, looking as if he might be dead.

"Oh, no!" thought Beauty. "What have I done?"

She immediately put the ring on her bedside table and was transported back to her chamber in the Beast's castle. She had never known where he spent his days and, though she searched the castle, she could not find him. Impatiently, she waited for supper time, and could not eat a thing because she expected the Beast at any minute. But he did not come.

Desperate, she rushed out into the grounds and,

remembering her dream, ran to the rose garden. And there he was, lying on the ground as if dead.

"Oh, it is all my fault!" cried Beauty, running to his side. She covered his hairy ugly face with kisses and wept over him. "Oh, my poor Beast, do not die! I should never forgive myself. Only live and I will marry you. For what do looks matter beside a kind and gentle heart?"

The Beast opened his eyes and—he was not a beast any more! Beauty found herself embracing a handsome young man. She jumped up in confusion. "Where is the Beast?" she cried.

"Here, Beauty," said the young man. "I was under an enchantment put upon me by a wicked fairy. I had to remain a beast until a beautiful young woman freely offered to marry me. You have saved me from the spell."

The two were happy as could be and Beauty's family were all brought to the castle in an instant. Beauty and her prince were married with great splendour, but her two sisters were turned into statues which had to stand at the gates, watching the young couple living happily, until their bad natures had turned to good. And I don't suppose that happened at all soon.

Cinderella

There was once a worthy man who was married to the best woman in the world. All her qualities of kindness, gentleness and beauty she left to her only daughter, Ella. That was the only legacy Ella had when her sweet mother died, for her father was short of money. He soon married again, and this time took a wealthy widow for his wife.

Ella's stepmother was as proud and vain as her real mother had been modest and unaffected. And, worst of all, she had two daughters of her own already, who took after her in their bad natures and cruel behaviour. As soon as the wedding was over, the stepmother took charge of the household. Ella was banished to a cold attic, with just a mattress on the floor, while her two stepsisters were given grand bedrooms with thick carpets, feather beds and full-length mirrors to admire themselves in.

For these two girls were as vain as their mother though, truth to tell, they had very little to be vain about, for their looks couldn't hold a candle to pretty little Ella's. The stepmother must have known this in her heart of hearts, because Ella annoyed her in every way, being docile and sweet when her own daughters were cross and rude, and always having a smile on her pretty face.

So the stepmother gave her all the worst household chores to do—taking out the rubbish, washing all the clothes till her little white hands were red and sore, and sweeping out the grates, so that her face was covered in smuts and her fine golden hair full of cinders.

"Lor, what a sight she is!" screamed her stepsisters. "We shall call her cinder-Ella!" and then they laughed till they cackled, so pleased were they with their wit.

Now, it happened that the king's son in that country decided to give a grand ball. All families of quality were invited, including Cinderella's. What a kerfuffle that caused in her household! The two stepsisters talked of nothing else for weeks except what they would wear and how they would do their hair. And Cinderella was such a

generous soul that she offered to do their hair for them.

And when the great day came, as she was combing and curling and brushing and arranging their hair, one of the stepsisters asked her, "Wouldn't you like to come to the ball yourself?"

"Very much," replied Cinderella, "but I should look out of place among fine ladies like yourselves."

"Quite right," said the other stepsister. "Who would want to see a dirty cindery creature like you in a ballroom?"

It says a lot for Cinderella's sweet nature that she didn't pull their hair or make it stick up in ugly tufts, but carried on with her task bravely and in silence.

But when the carriage had taken her father and his new family to the ball, she sank onto a kitchen chair and sobbed. Then, all of a sudden, her fairy godmother appeared and said to Cinderella, "Why are you crying, child?"

Cinderella was too upset to be surprised. "Because . . . because I should so like . . ." But she couldn't finish.

" . . . to go to the ball?" guessed her godmother, and Cinderella nodded.

"Then go to the ball you shall," she said.

"But I have nothing but rags to wear!" said Cinderella. "And how should I get there? My father has taken the carriage."

"Have you forgotten I'm a fairy?" asked her godmother. "Now, there's no time to lose. Go into the garden and fetch me a pumpkin from the vegetable patch."

Cinderella didn't stop to ask why. She ran into the garden and cut the biggest pumpkin, that she had been saving to make soup with, and brought it back to her godmother. The fairy took it into the courtyard, scraped it out till just the rind was left, then tapped it with her wand.

And there before Cinderella's eyes was a handsome gilded coach, fit for a princess. "Now, go and see if there are any mice in the mousetrap," said the fairy.

Cinderella found six white mice, all alive, and the fairy tapped each one, turning it into a fine grey horse. So now there was a team of horses to pull the coach. Cinderella clapped her hands.

"What shall we do for a coachman, Godmother? I know—I'll look for a rat in the rat trap."

And she brought her godmother a rat, with long whiskers. One tap of the fairy's wand turned him into a coachman with a particularly fine moustache. "Go and fetch me the six lizards you will find behind the water-butt," said the fairy and, when Cinderella had brought them to her, she turned them into six footmen in handsome shiny livery.

So now Cinderella had a very grand way of getting to the ball, but she was still standing in the courtyard in her rags.

"Now for you, my dear," said the fairy, and tapped Cinderella herself with the wand. In a trice, the poor

ragged girl was transformed into a princess, wearing a ballgown of gold and silver, her hair dressed in a beautiful style and her throat circled by diamonds. To finish off her outfit was a dainty pair of glass slippers.

"You will be the belle of the ball, said her godmother, as she handed Cinderella into the coach. "But I must warn you that, at midnight, everything will return to its usual shape and all your finery will disappear. You must be sure to leave the ball in good time."

"I will, Godmother," promised Cinderella. "And thank you for everything."

At the ball, the stepsisters were all of a flutter every time the prince danced past them. He was very good-looking and they both decided they would like him for a husband. While they were arguing about which of them he would ask to dance first, a beautiful and mysterious princess arrived in the ballroom.

No one knew who she was, perhaps a visitor from a foreign country? But the prince noticed her straightaway and from then on had eyes for no one else. He danced with Cinderella all evening, although she would not tell him her name or anything about herself. She had the most wonderful evening of her life. Her beauty had charmed the king himself, who gave her special sweetmeats from his own plate, which she took great pleasure in sharing with

her stepsisters. They, of course, did not recognise her.

Then there were more dances with the prince and the hours just flew by. Before she knew it, Cinderella heard the clock beginning to strike twelve. "Oh, no!" she thought, and she ran out of the ballroom so fast that she didn't even say goodbye to the prince. As she ran down the stairs to her coach, she lost one of her glass slippers, but had no time to pick it up.

And, of course, by the time she reached her coach, there was nothing to be seen but a pumpkin and some garden animals, and her splendid clothes had turned back to rags.

Poor Cinderella had to walk barefoot all the way home (she put the remaining glass slipper in her pocket). She was cold and tired by the time she got there and, not long afterwards, her stepsisters arrived home and wanted to tell her all about the ball.

Cinderella didn't have to pretend that she hadn't been anywhere; she looked so pale and tattered, no one would have guessed she had danced with a prince at a grand ball. Certainly not her stepsisters.

"Oh, you should have seen the fine dresses and jewels!" they said, as Cinderella unhooked, unlaced and removed all their finery.

"And one guest in particular," they said, "was

astonishingly beautiful and grand. She shared the king's sweetmeats with us."

Cinderella couldn't help smiling through her yawns.

The next morning, everyone was slow to get up, which was just as well, for poor Cinderella overslept, too. But her stepmother and stepsisters were all cross. Their tea was too cold, their toast too brown, their butter wouldn't spread and their napkins weren't folded properly.

But, in the middle of all their complaints, there came a loud knock on the door. It was a messenger from the prince. What a flutter that caused in the stepsisters' hearts! It seemed that the prince was sick with love for the mysterious princess and wanted to marry her. Since she had left behind one of her glass slippers, he had decreed that every young woman in the kingdom should try it on. The prince would marry the one it fitted. The messenger had been searching all night, but the slipper had fitted no one.

The stepsisters nearly fell over themselves in their haste

to try on the slipper. But it was no good. Their feet were so big, they couldn't squeeze in more than their toes. Just then, Cinderella stepped forward. "May I try it on?" she asked.

"The cheek of the girl!" fumed her stepmother, but the messenger looked at her pretty face and saw that, in spite of her rags, she might be the one.

"My orders are to let every young woman try it," he said.

So Cinderella slipped her foot into the little glass shoe. Imagine her stepsisters' surprise! And imagine their even greater surprise when she drew out the other slipper from her pocket and put that on, too!

At that moment, her fairy godmother appeared again and struck Cinderella with her wand, so that she was once more dressed in gorgeous clothes. Now the stepsisters recognised the grand "princess" of the night before.

She went back to the palace with the messenger and was reunited with the prince. Within a few days they were married and Cinderella, who had such a sweet nature and was so happy, found two courtiers of good family to marry her stepsisters. And it must be said that they were a great deal nicer when they were rich and married than they had been before. But Princess Ella was already as nice as she could be and so she always remained.

The Little Mermaid

In the middle of the furthest ocean, where the waters are deepest, live the Mer-people. Their home is beautiful with gardens and flowers, and the only difference between our landscape and this seascape is that fishes dart between the trees instead of birds.

The ancient palace of the Mer-king was made of coral, with amber windows and a roof of mussel shells, which opened and shut in the rippling water. The Mer-king himself had six beautiful daughters but no wife to help manage them. The Mer-princesses' mother had died years before and the household was managed by the king's mother.

Each princess had her own little garden and some were decorated with trophies from shipwrecks. The youngest princess, who was the most beautiful, had rescued the marble statue of a boy from a wrecked ship and put it in the middle of her garden. She was a quiet child and liked to sit and gaze at her statue.

She was very interested in humans and always eager

to hear what her grandmother had to tell her about life above the waves. As each princess reached the age of fifteen, she was allowed to visit the world above the sea, and the little mermaid couldn't wait for her turn.

When it was time for her oldest sister to swim above, the little mermaid was very excited and eager to hear all the news. When her sister returned, full of stories of the town she could see from the shore, its lights and music and the sound of its church bells, no one listened more intently than the youngest princess.

And so it was for the next five years, as each sister swam up to the surface and came back with stories of clouds and birds and ships and icebergs. The little mermaid felt that her turn would never come.

But of course, it did. On the evening of her fifteenth birthday, her grandmother called her over and adorned her hair with a wreath of white lilies made from pearls. To be truthful, the little mermaid would have preferred a simple garland of red flowers from her garden, but she understood that a princess must look grand at all times.

She said goodbye to all her sisters and rose alone through the blue waters of the ocean. The sun was setting as she broke through the surface of the water, and the sky was streaked with gold and rose. The evening star was shining and the sea was still as a looking-glass.

A large three-masted sailing ship was moving calmly through the ocean and the little mermaid could hear sweet music coming from it. As the sky grew dark, dozens of little lamps were lit on deck and coloured flags fluttered in the slight breeze. The mermaid thought she had never seen anything prettier.

So she swam closer and looked through the portholes.

There she saw a merry party of men dressed in rich velvets and satins, such as she had never seen. The handsomest of all was a young man not more than sixteen, and it seemed to be his birthday. Soon, all the men went up on deck and fireworks were let off. At first, the noise and gunpowdery smells terrified the mermaid and she hid under the water, but her curiosity got the better of her and then she thought she had never seen anything so wonderful. The whole sky was alight with green and gold and purple stars.

The little mermaid watched late until the party was over and everyone had gone to bed. Then she looked through the cabin porthole of the young man (who was, in fact, a prince) and gazed on him while he slept. His lovely face reminded her of her marble statue, but was made more beautiful by the colour in his lips and cheeks and the breath that stirred a feather on his pillow.

As the little mermaid followed the prince's ship, the waters below her began to heave and the sky to darken. A fierce wind whipped the waves into tall peaks and the rain fell heavily from the sky. The little mermaid loved it, especially when the ship went up and down in the water and the waves towered over it.

But the crew felt very differently. They scrambled to furl the sails, but they couldn't save the ship. It was struck by a huge wave and cracked in two. For the first time, the little mermaid realised that her prince was in danger.

She swam to the sinking ship, weaving between the broken spars, and looked everywhere for the young man. Then, a flash of lightning illuminated the scene, and she saw the prince clinging to a piece of wood. She swam to his side and pulled him out of the way of the ship,

which was now disappearing under the waves, taking many sailors with it.

The prince was half-dead, his eyes closed, and unaware of his rescuer, who held him in her arms till daybreak. When the sun came up, the little mermaid saw that they were near an island and swam towards the woody shore.

There was a little bay, where a river ran down to the sea, and the mermaid swam into it and pushed the prince onto the sandy shore, turning his face to the sun. But, of course, she couldn't get far out of the water because of her tail. As soon as she had done what she could for him, she hid among some reeds.

As the sun climbed higher, a group of girls came down from a white building to bathe in the river. The little

mermaid heard their exclamations as they found the prince. Their leader, a tall young woman, revived him and the little mermaid had the satisfaction of seeing him awake and speak, but then she became afraid of so many humans so near to her and dived back to her home beneath the waves.

But she could not forget the prince. She spent all her time in her garden, talking to her statue, until her family were quite worried about her. Eventually she told her secret to one of her sisters, who passed it on to the others.

They were all very sympathetic and told her they knew the country where the prince lived. They even took her to see his castle. From then on, she spent hours watching the castle and occasionally caught a glimpse of the prince.

Whenever she was under the water, she thought how dull her home looked, with its colours all blue and green and mauve, and she longed for the bright yellow of daffodils and sunshine and golden crowns.

The little mermaid wanted to know all she could about humans, so she went to her grandmother and asked, "If they do not drown, do human beings live forever?"

"No, my child," said her grandmother. "They all die, and they don't even live anything like as long as we do. We, as you know, live three hundred years. But then, sadly, we are turned to foam and cannot remain with our loved ones."

"What happens to humans, then?" asked the little mermaid.

"Their souls go on living after their bodies die," said her grandmother. "And in their heaven they are reunited with those they have loved on earth."

"Oh, how beautiful!" cried the little mermaid. "I should give up my three hundred years for one day as a human if I could have an immortal soul."

"Don't be so silly," said her grandmother. "We are far happier than humans are and enjoy our lives more than they do."

"Then is there no way," asked the little mermaid, "that a mer-person could get a human soul?"

"Well, there is," said her grandmother, reluctantly. "But it never happens. If a mermaid could get a human man to promise to love her and take her in marriage, then she would get a share of his soul. But the reason it won't happen is that the feature we admire most—our fine tails —is to humans most repulsive. They want a body to finish in two ugly pillars, which they call legs."

This gave the little mermaid lots to think about and, from then on, she was determined to get a pair of legs and make the prince love her as she loved him. There was an enchantress living under the sea, of whom all the mermaids were afraid, for she lived in a castle of human

bones in the middle of a boiling whirlpool.

But now the little mermaid determined to go and see her. She braved the bog and the trees made of living coils which snatched at passers-by, and made her way to the enchantress' throne. The sea-witch sat with a toad in her lap, caressing it as a fine lady would her cat.

"I know what you want," she told the little mermaid. "And you can have it, but at a price."

When the little mermaid heard what she would have to do to get legs, she nearly fainted.

"First, you must give up your beautiful voice to me," said the witch. "No more singing or even speaking for you."

The little mermaid agreed, though she was sad that her prince would never hear her silvery singing voice.

"Next, you must know that if I take away your tail and give you legs, the moment of transformation will be like having your tail cut in half by a sword. And every step you take upon the land will be like walking on knives."

"I would do anything for my prince," said the little mermaid, bravely.

"Very well," said the witch. "Now, finally, you must know that if the prince doesn't come to love you enough to marry you, then the morning after he marries another, your heart will break and you will turn into foam upon the sea. Are you sure that the slim chance of an immortal soul is worth all this suffering?"

"Yes," said the little mermaid. "My prince is worth all of it."

So the witch made her a terrible potion and took her voice away. She told the little mermaid to swim to the shore and drink the potion there.

The little mermaid swam away over her own palace, where all her family lay sleeping, and far away, carrying the phial, to the palace of the prince. There, she pulled herself up onto the shore and boldly drank the whole potion in one go.

Immediately, the terrible pains started in her tail. How she suffered as it split and shrank and she grew two slender legs in its place.

She shed a silent tear or two as she saw her glittery silver scales disappear. When she tried to stand, she thought the pain would kill her. Slowly, she dragged her unfamiliar legs, in spite of the sensation of walking on knives, until she found herself on the marble steps of the palace, where she fell into a swoon.

By then, it was morning and the palace guards found her. She was dressed in nothing but her long hair and some seaweed, but she was so beautiful that they were sure the prince would want to see her. So they took her to the housekeeper to be washed and dressed and then she was taken to the prince.

He was enchanted by her, though she could speak not a word, and asked her to dance with him. Imagine, if it caused her pain to walk, what agony it was for her to dance! But the little mermaid moved as gracefully as the waves and everyone admired her.

Soon she was the prince's firm favourite and she was as happy as could be. But, as time went by, he showed no signs of wanting to marry her. In fact, he began to treat her as if she were a pretty toy or a favourite pet.

The little mermaid asked the prince with her eyes if he loved her, and he understood and said, "Oh, I do love you, little one. You are so sweet and pretty. You remind me of a lovely maiden who rescued me from drowning. I was cast up on an island after a shipwreck and there was a temple full of maidens. One of them saved my life and sent me back to my country and I have dreamed of her ever since. You are a bit like her and, since I shall never find her again, you must be my comfort."

The little mermaid's eyes filled with unshed tears. He didn't even know that it was she who had saved him!

Next day, she heard the courtiers talking of the prince's forthcoming marriage to the daughter of a neighbouring king, but she didn't believe them.

But that night, the prince said to her as he curled a lock of her hair between his fingers, "I must go and see this princess my parents want me to marry. But she can't look as much like that temple maiden as you do, so I shan't marry her. Will you come with me? You aren't afraid of the sea, are you?" And the little mermaid shook her head and smiled.

But when they reached the land where the foreign princess lived, she became uneasy, for she recognised the shore. And indeed, as soon as the prince saw the princess, he recognised her.

"It is she, the temple maiden who saved my life!" he told his little companion. "Come, you must be happy for me—I know how fond of me you are."

And the little mermaid nodded, but her heart was hurting even more than her legs, which was an old pain she was used to. This new pain came from the knowledge that her prince would marry someone else and she would never gain an immortal soul.

The next day, the prince and his princess were married and he brought his bride on board his ship, a ship very like the one that the little mermaid had first seen him on. Again, there were lights and music and fireworks, but how different they seemed to the little mermaid. She leaned on the rail, knowing that at the first rays of the rising sun, she would be turned into foam.

Looking down in the water, she suddenly saw her five sisters swimming alongside the ship. But they were different; their lovely long hair was all cut off.

"We gave it to the sea-witch!" they cried, "in return for a spell to save you. You must take this dagger and plunge it into the prince's heart before daybreak. Then let his warm blood fall on your feet and your mermaid's tail will be restored. Then you can live with us for your full three hundred years. But you must act before morning; either you or he must die. Farewell! Then they plunged under the waves.

The mermaid took the dagger they had given her and went into the prince's cabin. She saw him sleeping peacefully and she knew she could never hurt him. She ran to the edge of the ship and

threw the dagger
in the water. Just then,
the red beams of the rising
sun streaked the sky. With a
voiceless cry, the little mermaid
leapt over the edge of the ship and
felt herself dissolving into foam.

But, as she sank below the
water, she saw the sky filled with
transparent beings, with sweet melodious
voices. They swept down and took the
little mermaid up with them and she saw
that she had become as transparent as
they were. They were spirits of the air
and they gave her her
voice back.

So the mermaid went singing through the air with her companions. She was able to swoop down and kiss her prince, unseen, as he looked sorrowfully over the side of the ship for her. Then she travelled through the air for three hundred years, with the spirits, doing good deeds and bringing happiness everywhere.

And, because she had loved so much and so hard, at the end of that time she won an immortal soul for herself, long after the prince and his descendants were turned to dust.

The Six Swans

A king was once out hunting in the forest when he chased his quarry so far and fast that he went out of his companions' sight. He lost the beast but—which was worse—he found that he had lost himself, too. He wandered around the forest on horseback and on foot and could find no path to take him out of it again.

He would surely have been lost for ever, had he not come across a bent old woman who said she could show him the way home. But she had a condition: the king was to marry her daughter in return. A ridiculous bargain to make with a king, you might say, but a king can starve just as easily as an ordinary man and this king believed he had no choice.

So he went with the woman to her hut and was introduced to her daughter. She was a good-looking young woman and the king had lost his own dear wife. Yet there was something he didn't quite like about her. Still, he had made the bargain, so he put the young woman on his horse and her old mother led them both out of the forest.

Within a few days, the king and the forest-girl were married. But he didn't tell her about his children. The king had six sons and a daughter by his first wife but, as soon as he had brought his new wife back to the palace, he had them moved to a castle some distance away. He had a feeling that they would not be safe with the girl from the forest.

The castle was so cleverly concealed in the depths of another forest that it was very difficult to find. But a wise woman had given the king a ball of string with magical properties. Whenever the king threw it to the ground, it unrolled in the direction of the castle and showed him how to get there.

The king went to visit his children so often that his absences made his wife suspicious. She bribed his servants to tell her where he went and gave them so much money that they also told her about the ball of string and showed her where it was kept.

The queen made six shirts of white silk and, using spells she had learned from her mother, sewed a magic charm into each one. Then she waited till the king had gone hunting, stole the ball of string and set off for the castle.

The children saw someone coming from a distance and, since they thought it was their father, the boys ran out to meet him. But the girl stopped to tidy her game away. So she was still indoors when the boys realised it wasn't their father, but a strange woman. And she was throwing white shirts over their heads.

As soon as the shirts touched their skin, the six princes were changed into swans, who swooped up and away into the air. The queen went back to the palace well satisfied that she had got rid of her stepchildren. But she didn't know about the king's daughter. Perhaps the servants hadn't mentioned her? After all, the queen had made only six shirts.

The next day, the king went to visit his children and found his daughter on her own. "Where are your brothers?" he asked.

"I don't know," said his daughter. "They have flown away." And she told him what she had seen from the window, and showed him some white swan's feathers that she had found in the courtyard.

The king was horrified, but he did not suspect that the woman with the shirts had been his wife. He wanted to take his daughter back to the palace to live with them, but the little girl was scared of

her stepmother and begged to be left in the castle another day.

When he had gone, the girl decided she would go and look for her brothers. She walked all night long and all the next day, but then she was too tired to go on. She came to a hut in the forest and went inside. There were six beds in it and she crawled under one of them and fell asleep.

It was sunset and, suddenly, the hut was full of the sound of swishing wings. Six white swans came flying in through the window. They landed on the ground and blew at one another till all their feathers fell off. They were revealed to be the girl's six brothers.

She came out from her hiding place and fell upon them with joy. They were so pleased to see her.

"But you can't stay here," they said. "This house belongs to robbers and they will come back. Then they will kill you."

"But you will save me, brothers, surely?" said the girl.

"We won't be able to," they told her. "We can keep our human forms for only a quarter of an hour each day. After that we have to be swans again."

Their sister cried for them. "Is there no way to set you free from the spell?"

"There is a way," they said, "but it is too hard for anyone. For six years you must not open your mouth to say a single word. In that time, you must sew six shirts out of starwort and, if you put them on us, we will return to our human forms. But if you say a single word, all that work will be in vain."

At that moment, their quarter of an hour was up and they became swans again and flew out of the window.

But the girl had made up her mind. She went out into the forest again and started to collect starwort, so that she could start making the shirts.

In this way, she led her life for a long time, speaking to no one. Then, one day, the king of another country came riding through the forest and saw her sitting under a tree. He was struck by her great beauty.

"Who are you," he asked. "What is your name and where do you come from?"

But the girl answered not a word. Still, she liked the king and, when he said he would like to take her back to his palace, she agreed by nodding. The king took the girl home with him and dressed her in fine clothes in which she looked every inch a princess. But she still never spoke a word.

She collected starwort and stitched the shirts steadily and faithfully, though she was glad to do it in a palace rather than in the forest. And she soon came to love the king, who was so kind and loving to her. Soon, he asked her to marry him and again she nodded.

They would have been happy, in spite of the lack of conversation, but for one thing. The king's mother was a spiteful nasty woman and she was terribly against the marriage. "You know nothing about her," she told her son. "You found her in the forest but know nothing of where she comes from. She cannot speak, so how can she be worthy of a king?"

After a year, the young queen gave birth to a child and the wicked old queen waited till she was sleeping, then stole the baby and smeared animal blood on the sleeping mother's mouth. When this was discovered, everyone was horrified, but the king refused to believe that his gentle wife could have harmed their child.

Another year passed and the same thing happened. The young queen had another baby and the old queen stole it away and smeared the mother's mouth with blood. Again, the king refused to believe the evidence, though his heart was aching.

But he couldn't ignore it when it happened a third time, a year later. Their third child was born and stolen by the old queen. The king was heartbroken to think that he had lost his third child. But, if he was unhappy, think how his poor wife was suffering! She had lost all her children, been accused of the most wicked behaviour, and she couldn't say a word in her defence.

The king sadly agreed that his wife must be burned at the stake. As she was led out, she carried the six shirts with her, for the six years was up that very day. She just hadn't quite managed to finish the left sleeve of the smallest shirt.

As she was being bound to the stake, she saw six white swans come wheeling through the air. It was her brothers! She threw the shirts over them and they were all restored to human form. And then her lips were opened and she poured forth her story: what had happened to her brothers; her vow of silence; her love for her husband and her lost children; and her suspicions of her mother-in-law.

The king ordered his mother to tell the truth and she sent for the three royal babies, who had not been harmed. The king and his queen were delighted to have their children back and the young queen was so happy to have her brothers back. But the youngest brother had a swan's wing instead of his left arm, because that shirt had not been quite finished.

The wicked queen was tied to the stake, instead of the innocent young queen, and burned to ashes. But the king and queen and their three children lived happily ever after, with the six brothers who had been swans.

The Frog Prince

Long, long ago, when wishing was useful, there lived a
king with a very beautiful daughter. She was so used
to everyone telling her that she was lovely as the day that,
to be truthful, she had become rather vain and silly and
inclined to think that everyone should do as she said.

By the castle was an old dark forest and, at the edge of
it, in the castle grounds, was a tall shady lime tree. Under
the lime tree was a well of clear cool water beside which
the princess liked to sit, playing with her golden ball.

One day, she was sitting by the well tossing the ball up

in the air and catching it, tossing it up and catching it, tossing it up and . . . oh! dropping it down the deep, deep well! The princess sprang to the rim of the well and looked down, but it was no good. She couldn't even see the bottom, let alone her golden ball. How she wept and wailed!

"What's the matter, princess?" said a deep voice. "You cry so hard that even a stone would have pity on you."

The princess looked up and saw a large frog sticking his big ugly head out of the well.

"Alas," she said, through her tears. "I have dropped my golden ball down the well and it is so deep that I shall never get it back."

"Don't say that," said the frog. "I could get your plaything for you, but I'd want something in return."

"Anything!" said the princess, clapping her hands and quite cheerful again. "My clothes, my jewels, why, even my little golden crown."

"Pah!" said the frog. "What good are such things to me? I can't wear your clothes or your jewels and a frog would look silly in a crown. What I want is for you to love me and let me be your companion. Will you let me eat off your golden plate and drink from your golden cup and sleep in your golden bed?"

"Yes, yes, of course," said the princess, impatiently.

"Anything you want. Only do hurry and fetch me my ball."

The frog disappeared into the water in a shower of bubbles and was back in a trice, carrying the ball in his wide mouth. He spat it out on the grass and the princess, delighted to have her plaything back, wiped it on her silk gown and skipped back to the castle to change her clothes.

And did she thank the frog? No. Did she remember her promise to him? No. The poor frog hopped wetly after her, crying, "Wait for me, wait for me!" while the princess never even looked back.

As she was sitting down to supper with the king her father, there came the strangest sound, of something creeping splish, splash, splish, splash, up the grand marble staircase. There was a knock at the dining-room door and a deep voice said, "Princess, princess, let me in!"

Startled, the princess opened the door, but shut it again

quickly when she saw the lumpy bumpy face of the frog looking up at her. She went back to her place with a racing heart and flushed face.

"Why, whatever is the matter, my dear?" asked the king. "Is there a giant outside the door?"

"No, Father, it is not a giant, but just a disgusting old frog."

"A frog, my dear? What does a frog want with you?"

"Today, my golden ball fell in the well and the frog got it back for me. And . . . and he made me promise he could be my companion in return. But I didn't imagine he could leave the well. And now here the horrid thing is."

And she started to cry some very small crystal tears which just wet her long lashes and made her eyes look pretty. But, to her astonishment, her father gave her a very stern look.

"A promise is a promise," said the king. "No matter to whom you make it."

And he made the princess open the door and let the frog in. The frog hopped slowly up to the table, for he was tired after his long journey from the well.

"Lift me up beside you," he cried.

The princess shuddered, but her father was still watching her seriously, so she did as the frog asked. Her lumpy bumpy new companion pushed his mouth into her golden plate and dipped his long tongue into her cup. And, strangely, the princess lost all her appetite and ate and drank no more of her supper.

When the frog was full, he said to the princess, "I am very tired. Now take me to your bedroom and let us both lie in your golden bed."

At this, the princess began to cry in earnest, for she hated the idea of the cold wet frog in her clean and comfortable bed. But the king was angry with her. "The frog kept his side of the bargain," he said. "Now you must keep yours."

So the princess held the frog at arm's length, from the tips of her fingers, and carried him to her room, where she put him in a corner. Then she went to bed and cried herself to sleep.

She was woken by the clammy frog trying to climb into her bed.

"Lift me up!" he said, "or I shall tell your father."

So she did.

"Now, princess, if you are my loving companion, as you promised," said the frog, "you must kiss me goodnight."

How the princess screwed up her pretty eyes so that she might not see him and how she screwed up her pretty nose that she might not smell him and how she screwed up her pretty mouth that she might not taste him! And she gave the frog the quickest little peck of a kiss that she could get away with.

There was a rushing sound in the room and, when the princess opened her eyes, there was no frog to be seen.

Instead of his ugly warty face, there gazed back at her the handsomest prince she had ever seen!

Immediately, he went down on one knee.

"Thank you, thank you, beautiful princess," he said. "You have broken the spell. A witch changed me into a frog and condemned me to live in that cold dark well, until a beautiful princess released me with a kiss."

Imagine the princess's confusion! But her father had told her she must be a loving companion to the frog. So the princess suddenly discovered she was very obedient and married her frog prince and lived happily ever after.

You Can't Catch Me,
I'm the Gingerbread Man

Nonsense Stories

The Three Sillies

There was once a farmer and his wife who had a very pretty daughter. But although she was pleasing to look at, she was not very clever—and this was not surprising, for her parents were not very clever either. But this foolish pretty girl was being courted by a gentleman, who came for supper at the farmhouse every evening.

It was the girl's job to go down to the cellar and draw a jug of beer from the barrel that was kept down there. One evening, when she was doing this, her attention

wandered and she noticed a
mallet wedged in the rafters
above her head.

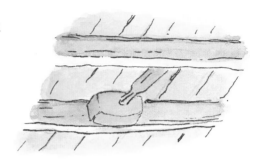

"Oh, wouldn't it be
terrible," said the girl to
herself, "if I married and my husband and I had a son and
he grew up and came down here to draw some beer and
that mallet fell on his head and killed him?"

And she was so upset by this dreadful idea that she sat
down on the floor and threw her apron over her head and
began to howl. After a while she was missed upstairs and
her mother came to look for her. She found the beer
running out of the barrel all over the floor and her
daughter in floods of tears.

"Why, whatever's the matter?" exclaimed the mother.

"Only think, Ma," sobbed the foolish girl. "Suppose I
got married and we had a son and he grew up and came
down here to draw beer. There's a horrid old mallet up
there in the rafters and it might fall down on his head and
kill him stone dead!"

As soon as the mother had heard this awful suggestion,
she, too, sat down and threw her apron over her head and
began to cry just as loudly as her daughter.

"I can't think what has happened to the women," said the farmer. "They're taking an awfully long time to draw a jug of beer. I'd best go down and see what's keeping them."

And when he got down into the cellar, the farmer saw his wife and daughter sitting with their aprons over their heads and crying fit to bust, while the beer ran all over the floor.

"What on earth has happened?" he asked, in some alarm.

"Why, husband," wept his wife. "The most terrible thing. Look at that mallet stuck in the rafters! Suppose our daughter married her suitor and they had a son and he grew up and came down here to draw beer and that horrid mallet fell on his head and killed him!"

"That's awful!" said the farmer and he sat down beside them and burst into tears, too, at the thought of his grandson's fate. The gentleman had been left all

alone upstairs and soon became
anxious about what had
happened to the family, so
he went down into the
cellar to find them.

Imagine his
surprise at
finding all
three sitting
on the floor,
which was awash with
beer, crying their eyes out! He stepped quickly to the
barrel and turned the tap off.

"Will someone please tell me what is going on?"

"Alas," said the farmer. "Do you see yonder mallet
stuck in the rafters? Suppose you marry my daughter and
the two of you have a son and he grows up and comes
down here to draw beer and that mallet falls on his head
and kills him? Isn't that cause enough for grief?"

The gentleman could hardly speak for laughing. He
went over to the mallet and pulled it out of the rafters and
set it on a shelf.

"Dry your eyes, all of you. You really are the three

silliest people I have ever met! Now I am going on my travels and if I can find three people sillier than you, I shall come back and marry your daughter."

With that, he left the three sillies crying just as hard, because the girl had lost her sweetheart. He hadn't travelled far, before he saw an old woman trying to persuade her cow to climb a ladder.

"Why are you trying to get your cow up the ladder?" he asked.

"Why, I want her to eat the grass growing on the roof of my cottage," said the old woman. "It's a shame to waste it. And she'll be quite safe because when I've got her up, I'll tie this string round her neck and pass it down the chimney and fasten it round my waist."

"But wouldn't it be easier just to cut the grass and throw it down to the cow?" the gentleman couldn't help saying.

The old woman took no notice of this suggestion and the gentleman travelled on. But he heard a shriek behind him and turned to see that the cow had been hoisted onto the roof. It had slipped and fallen back down to the ground, yanking the old woman up the chimney!

The gentleman laughed so hard at the sight of the old woman on the roof all covered in soot shaking her fist at the cow, who was now munching the grass in her garden, that he nearly fell off his horse.

"Well, there is one person sillier than my sweetheart and her parents," he thought.

He travelled on and found an inn in which to rest. He had to share a room with another traveller, a very pleasant man, who was a good companion. But in the morning, this fellow-traveller did something very strange.

He hung his trousers on the doorknob, then went to the other side of the room and took a run at them, trying to jump into them! He did the same thing several times, till he was sweating with the effort, while the gentleman looked on in astonishment.

The man mopped his brow. "These trousers are the invention of the devil!" he panted. "It always takes at least an hour to get into them. However do you manage to get dressed so quickly?"

So the gentleman showed him the easy way to put on trousers, though he could hardly do so for laughing. As he went on his way the gentleman thought, "There is another person sillier than my sweetheart and her parents."

He travelled to a village where there was a crowd of people gathered round the pond, with rakes and brooms and sticks.

"What's up?" he asked one of them.

"Nay, rather ask what's down," said the villager, "for

look—the moon's fallen into the pond and we can't get it out."

In vain did the gentleman point up at the sky to show them that the moon was still there and that what was in the pond was just a reflection. The villagers didn't want to know and sent him on his way with many insults.

"Why," thought the gentleman. "There are many more sillies in this world than my pretty sweetheart and her good parents."

And he rode back to the farm and asked the farmer's daughter to marry him straightaway. Which she did, and if they are not happy still, it is not my business or yours.

The Gingerbread Man

Once upon a time a farmer's wife made a batch of gingerbread and with a leftover piece she shaped a little man. You might not think this unusual, because you can see gingerbread men in any baker's window, but this one was the very first such man that had ever been made.

The farmer's wife gave him raisins for eyes and, when he was baked and cooled, she took her icing bag and gave him a bow tie, a mouth and three buttons down his front.

"What a handsome fellow you are!" she exclaimed. "It will be a shame to eat you."

"Eat me!" cried the gingerbread man, sitting up on the baking tray. "No fear—I'm off!"

And he jumped off the table and ran out of the kitchen door. At first the farmer's wife was too astonished to move but, when she saw her sweet treat running away, she set off after him. But he just called out:

"Run, run, fast as you can,

You can't catch me—I'm the Gingerbread Man!"

He had soon put the farm far behind him and found himself in a village. He was running past the butcher's shop when the butcher caught sight of him.

"Stop, let me eat you," cried the butcher.

But the gingerbread man just kept running, calling back over his shoulder:

"Run, run, fast as you can,

You can't catch me—I'm the Gingerbread Man!"

He ran past the blacksmith's and the blacksmith himself came out to look. When he saw the gingerbread man, his mouth watered and he gave chase. But the little man ran on, crying:

"Run, run, fast as you can,

You can't catch me—I'm the Gingerbread Man!"

A little while later he came to the flour mill and the miller ran out to catch him. "Stop, stop!" cried the miller, "I want to eat you up!"

Well, of course, that made the gingerbread man run faster, calling out:

"Run, run, fast as you can,

You can't catch me—I'm the Gingerbread Man!"

By now he was outside the village and running across a field, where he was spotted by a very surprised cow. He nearly ran into her mouth as she munched the grass. She caught a whiff of his delicious smell and started to lumber after him, mooing in such a way that he knew what she intended.

So he ran even faster, crying out to the cow:

"Run, run, fast as you can,

You can't catch me—I'm the Gingerbread Man!"

Now he was in the horse's field and the horse came to

investigate him. "Neigh!" said the horse. "You look tasty. Stop and let me try you."

So the gingerbread man started to sprint, crying:

"Run, run, fast as you can,

You can't catch me—

I'm the Gingerbread Man!"

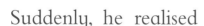

Suddenly, he realised that he could go no further. There was a stream at the bottom of the field and the horse was behind him. But there was a handsome red fox grooming himself on the bank of the stream and he offered to ferry the gingerbread man across.

The fox was the only being the gingerbread man had met that morning who hadn't wanted to eat him, so he took hold of the fox's tail and the fox started to swim across the stream. Halfway across he said to the gingerbread man, "I am afraid you will get wet. Climb onto my back." So the gingerbread man did.

Three quarters of the way across the stream, the fox said, "I am still afraid you will get wet. Why not climb onto my head?" So the gingerbread man did.

And when they were nearly at the opposite bank, the fox said, "This is the awkward bit. When I get out of the water I have to shake my fur. If you climb onto my nose you will stay dry."

So the gingerbread man climbed onto the fox's nose.

And then the fox flipped up his long red nose, opened his big greedy mouth and swallowed the gingerbread man up in one bite!

And that was the end of the first gingerbread man. Many of them have been made and eaten since and I shouldn't wonder if you've had one yourself.

The Magic
Porridge Pot

There was once a little girl who lived with her mother and they had very little money. The day came when the money ran out altogether and they had nothing to eat.

The mother sat weeping, with her apron over her head, but the little girl went for a walk thinking she might find an answer to their problem. And so she did, for wandering in the forest she met an old woman who gave her a little cooking pot.

Somehow the old woman had guessed the child's problem. "Whenever you are hungry," she said, "put the pot on the stove and say, 'Cook, little pot, cook,' and it will be filled with good sweet porridge. When you want it to stop, say, 'Stop, little pot, stop,' and it will leave off cooking."

So their problems were over. The little girl and her mother never went hungry. Whenever they wanted food the magic pot filled them with nourishing porridge and if they ever fancied sausages or doughnuts, well they never mentioned it.

One day when the little girl was out, her mother said the words, "Cook, little pot, cook!" and the magic pot started to bubble with porridge. When it was full, the mother wanted it to stop, but she couldn't remember what words to use. So the porridge boiled up over the rim of the pot and soon filled the whole kitchen. Then it poured right out of the door and down the path and still the pot kept cooking. It filled the next door house with porridge and the next and the next until the whole row of houses was

full of boiling hot porridge.

It was as if the pot wanted to feed everyone in the village. Soon there was only one house left that wasn't full of porridge and all the villagers were crowded into it.

At that moment the little girl came home. Or tried to. As soon as she saw the river of porridge running down the street, she knew what had happened. She ran to where the shape of her house could be seen under its overcoat of porridge and cried, "Stop, little pot, stop!"

Immediately the magic pot left off cooking and anyone who wanted to get back into their house had to eat a lot of porridge. The mother promised never to use the pot again, but I think she must have been a very silly woman not to remember the words to stop it, don't you?

Sip and her Sisters

Once upon a time there was a king with three daughters. The oldest was called Sip. The next oldest was called Sipsippernip. And the third and youngest daughter was called Sipsippernipsipsirumsip.

In the neighbouring country there was another king who had three sons. The oldest son was called Skrat. The second was called Skratskratterat. And the third and youngest son was called Skratskratteratskratskirumskrat.

One day the first king went to have tea with the other

one and introduced his daughters to the other king's sons.

They got on famously. And in a short while the three princesses were engaged to the three princes.

Their wedding day came and this was how it was:

Sip got Skrat,

Sipsippernip got Skratskratterat,

and Sipsippernipsipsirumsip got

Skratskratteratskratskirumskrat.

What do you think of that?

The Princess
and the Pea

There was once a prince who decided he must have a wife, but the only wife that would do for him was what he called "a real princess". However, he didn't seem at all sure what that meant. Still, as he searched for one, he became more certain about who was *not* a real princess.

The prince travelled from country to country and found lots of princesses but there was always something wrong with them. One was too tall, one had bandy legs, one ate nothing but salad, one had a passion for wearing yellow, one beat her servants, one read nothing but romantic novels.

It seemed as if there was not one princess in this world good enough to marry the prince and he went back to his own castle very disappointed.

Then, one night, there was a terrible storm, with

 thunder and lightning and torrential rain. And at the height of the storm there came a knocking at the castle door. The servant who opened it found a very bedraggled young woman on the doorstep. Her clothes stuck to her body and water ran down her pretty face and hair in streams.

"Please give me shelter," she said. "And, by the way, I am a real princess."

Everyone in the castle had come to see who was at the door on such an awful night. There she stood, calm and dignified and sopping wet. "Can this be a real princess?" wondered the prince.

His mother, the queen, had an idea of her own about that. "Come in and warm yourself, my dear," she said, and ordered servants to prepare her a hot bath and fetch her dry clothes. And while all this was going on, the queen had the best guest bedroom prepared in a most unusual way.

The bed was stripped and one dried pea placed on the bedstead. Then twenty mattresses were piled on top of it and cotton sheets and a big fluffy duck-down duvet. If the princess thought her bed at all odd when she came to get in it, she said nothing. She merely climbed the handy ladder that had been provided and settled down to sleep.

The next morning the princess appeared at breakfast with dark circles under her eyes.

"How did you sleep?" asked the queen.

"Very badly, ma'am," said the princess. "I'm sorry to say it but my bed was very uncomfortable. I felt there was something hard and sharp underneath me and I tossed and turned all night."

"A real princess at last!" cried the prince, clapping his hands. "Only a royal lady of the utmost refinement could have felt that pea under twenty mattresses."

And he went down on one knee and asked her to marry him on the spot. Perhaps it was lucky for him that she was not searching for a perfect prince. Anyway, what is certain is that marry they did, and they lived together all the days of their lives. And the pea was preserved in a glass case in a museum and, if it is still there, you may see it to this day.

The Three Wishes

There was once an old woodcutter who was working in the forest. He had his bottle of water and his hunk of bread with him so that he could work all day. Well, as time went by, the woodcutter came to a big old oak tree.

He spat on his hands, picked up his axe and took a swing at the tree trunk. Then he heard a tiny voice saying, "Oh, please don't cut down my home!" and there was a little tree fairy standing at the foot of the great oak.

How she wept and pleaded with him till the old woodcutter, who had never seen a fairy before and was mightily taken with her, thought, "Well, there are plenty of other trees in the forest."

"All right, little one," he said. "I'll not cut your tree."

"Thank you, thank you," said the fairy. "And to show how grateful I am, I shall grant you and your wife your next three wishes." Then she disappeared.

The woodcutter carried on with his work and then went back to his hut, thinking that he must have dreamed what had happened.

"Hullo, wife," he called. "Is my supper ready, for I am mortal hungry."

"No, husband," said his wife. "It won't be ready for another hour."

The woodcutter sat down in his chair and sighed, for he had had nothing but his bread and water since breakfast and it had only been a little bowl of porridge then.

"I wish I had a fine big sausage," he said.

And lo and behold! A savoury, juicy, cooked sausage fell down the chimney!

"What on earth is going on?" asked his wife, very alarmed, for no sausage had ever come tumbling down her chimney before.

Then the woodcutter remembered his "dream". "It must be that fairy's doing," he said, and told his wife the whole story. She was so cross when she realised what had happened.

"What kind of fool are you?" she asked her husband. "You might have wished for gold or a fine house or a carriage, but no—you had to wish for a common or garden sausage such as I might get at the butchers any day. You are such an idiot that I wish that sausage was on your nose!"

And immediately the sausage flew out of the grate and fastened itself to the woodcutter's nose. No matter how he tugged, it would not come off, for it was stuck by magic and that is stronger than any glue.

The woodcutter realised that he was going to have to use his third wish to get the sausage off.

Especially when his wife started to say that it didn't look too bad! Quickly, he made a wish and the sausage came off.

Well, the woodcutter and his wife didn't have any gold or a fine house or carriage. But they did have a big, savoury, juicy sausage and it would have been a shame to waste it. So they sat down and ate it all up. The woodcutter has always kept his eyes open for tree fairies ever since, but he has never been lucky enough to see another one.

Turn Again, Whittington

Resourceful
Heroes
and Heroines

East o' the Sun and West o' the Moon

Once upon a time there was a large family who lived in the cold north. There were so many children that the mother and father were at their wits' end about how to feed and clothe them. The youngest child was a daughter and, although she never had anything to wear but hand-me-downs, which were more like rags by the time they reached her, she was very beautiful.

Then one day—it was a Thursday in autumn, by the

way, when the warmer weather (which wasn't very warm) was coming to an end—a huge white bear came to the poor family's hut. When the father opened the door, he was terrified to see the bear, but the bear said very politely that he had come to ask for the youngest daughter's hand in marriage.

"If you give your daughter to me," he said, "you will never know poverty or hunger again."

"Hold on a moment," said the man. "I'll ask."

And he went to find his youngest daughter.

"A white bear is here," he said. "He wants to marry you and, if you say yes, we'll all be rich."

"No," said the girl. "I don't want to marry a bear."

So the man went back to the door and told the bear the answer.

"Don't decide so fast," said the bear. "I'll come back in a week."

Well, that week the weather turned bitter cold and the

firewood ran out and there was no money for food, so all they had to eat was cold porridge. So when the bear came back, the daughter agreed to marry him.

The white bear put her on his back and ran away with her so fast it was like flying.

"Are you afraid?" he asked.

"No," she said, burying her face in his thick warm fur.

The bear took her to his castle inside a mountain of ice. The rooms were decorated in silver and gold and he gave the girl a silver bell to ring if she wanted anything.

She had only to think of something—like a good hot meal or a warm cloak—and ring her bell, and it was there. In the evening she became sleepy and wished for a bed. Immediately she was shown into a bedroom, made ready for her with silk hangings and a bed of goose down. The girl changed into the nightdress laid out for her and fell fast asleep.

The next day was the same. She wanted for nothing but company, since she saw nothing of the bear. But at night-time, she felt a man come and lie in her bed beside her. In the morning, he had gone before it was daylight. And so it went on for some months.

In spite of her new rich diet, the girl became pale and thin. She was lonely and very much missed her big family. She decided to ring the bell and ask to see the white bear.

In he shambled. "What is it you want, my dear?" he asked. "Are you not comfortable in my palace?"

"Very comfortable, bear, dear," she said. "But oh, so lonely. I miss my mother and father and my brothers and sisters. May I go on a visit to them?"

The bear could not refuse her, but he gave her some advice. "When you visit your family, you must not let your mother speak to you alone. She will try to, but you must not agree to be on your own with her."

The girl agreed and the bear let her climb on his back again to take her to her family. Of course they lived in a different house now, much more comfortably. How happy the girl was to see her family again! And they were very pleased to see her and to show her all their bedrooms with

fur coverlets and their dining-room with its table covered with good food and wine. It was quite unlike the old days.

When they had eaten, the mother tried to spend some time alone with her daughter, but the girl said no, there was no need.

"A girl needs a word or two alone with her mother when

she is to be married," said the mother. And the girl couldn't refuse her.

When they were alone, the mother asked all sorts of questions about her life with the bear and the girl said that she hadn't seen much of him.

"But every night a man comes and lies in my bed and I have never seen his face because he always leaves before daybreak."

"Then you must take this candle and flint and the next time he comes to you, you must stay awake and light the candle so that you can see him," advised her mother.

The girl took the candle and the flint and returned home with the white bear to his palace. That night, when her visitor came, she stayed awake and lit the candle. She found herself looking at the handsomest young man she had ever seen. Straightaway she fell in love with him. She leaned over to kiss him.

But three drops of wax from the candle fell on his shirt and woke him up. When he saw the girl, he cried out, "Alas! Why didn't you take my advice? I am the white bear who was to have married you. If you had stayed with me a year without trying to find out who I was, my enchantment would have been over. My stepmother bewitched me into being a bear by day and a man by night and you could have saved me. But now I must marry the troll-princess with a nose a metre long!"

The girl wept and wailed for she had now fallen in love with the prince. "Is there nothing I can do?" she cried.

"Nothing," said the prince. "All I can tell you is that she lives in a palace East o' the Sun and West o' the Moon."

At that moment, the ice-palace disappeared and the girl found herself sitting on the grass on the mountainside, wearing only her night gown. But she didn't give a thought to her own comfort, only to how she might find her prince again.

She set out on the road until she came to a lofty crag where an old woman sat playing with a golden apple.

"Please can you tell me the way to the palace that is East o' the Sun and West o' the Moon?" asked the girl.

"Why do you want to know?" asked the old woman. "Could it be that you are the one who should have married the white bear?"

"Yes," said the girl sadly, "I was."

"Well, I don't know where the palace is, but you may take my horse and ride to my sister. Just give him a tap under the left ear when you get there and he'll come back to me."

And the old woman gave the girl not only her horse but the golden apple she had been playing with. The girl

rode for a long weary time, until
she came to another crag, and
there was another old woman
using a golden carding comb.
She dismounted and asked, "Excuse
me, but your sister said you might know
the way to East o' the Sun and West o' the Moon?"

"Well I don't, but why would you want to know that.
Could it be that you are the one who should have married
the white bear?"

"Yes," said the girl sadly, "that's me."

"Then borrow my horse and ride to our other sister.
You may give him a tap under the left ear to send him
home. And you can take this golden carding comb. It
might come in useful."

So the girl mounted the fresh horse and rode even
further, till she was quite exhausted.
They arived at another crag where
there was a third old woman, who
looked just like the other
two. She was using a golden
spinning-wheel.

"Oh, please tell me if you

know the way to East o' the Sun and West o' the Moon," said the poor girl. "Your sisters sent me."

"Why would you want to know that, unless you are the girl who should have married the white bear?" said the old woman.

"Yes, yes, I should," sobbed the girl. "Do you know the way?"

"No, I don't. But take my horse and ride him till you come to the East Wind. Just give him a tap under the left ear and he'll trot back to me. And you may take this golden spinning-wheel, too."

So the girl, carrying the apple, the carding comb and the spinning-wheel, climbed onto the third horse and rode till she could ride no more. Fortunately that brought her to where the East Wind's house was.

Now, he knew no more than the old women where the palace was, but he said he would carry her on his back to his brother, the West Wind.

"He's much stronger than me and he might know where East o' the Sun and West o' the Moon may be."

The girl climbed onto the East Wind's back and if she had thought the white bear travelled fast, now she found out what speed really meant. But when they got to the West Wind's house, they had no luck.

"I don't know where East o' the Sun and West o' the Moon is," he said, "but I'll take you to my brother, the South Wind if you like. He's stronger than either of us."

So off she went again, whirling through the sky on the back of the West Wind.

The South Wind didn't know where the palace was either, but he was willing to take her to the North Wind—"He is the strongest of us all."

The girl was quite giddy by the

time they arrived at the North
Wind's house, but she felt worse
when the North Wind came out to
greet them.

"Blast you both!" he said
crossly, huffing and puffing. "What do you want?"

"Is that any way to talk to visitors?" said the South
Wind. "This is the girl who should have married the white
bear and she needs to find the palace that is East o' the
Sun and West o' the Moon. Can you help her?"

"Well, I have been there once," said the North Wind,
grumpily. "It was a long way and it
took all my strength. But I suppose
I could take her there."

The girl was very much afraid to
climb on the back of the rude North
Wind but she knew it was her best
chance, so she did. She flew through

the air with him, over storms and seas and out over the wildest oceans, until she felt that surely they had reached the end of the world.

At last the North Wind ran out of strength and drooped his wings and brought the girl to a far shore, under the windows of the palace that lay East o' the Sun and West o' the Moon. He had to rest for many days before he could make the return journey.

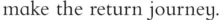

Next morning, the girl sat under the palace window playing with the golden ball. An ugly face with a nose a metre long looked out of the window.

"What do you want for that golden ball?" called the troll-princess (for that's who it was).

"It's not for sale," said the girl calmly, "at least not for money. But you can have it if you bring me to the prince."

"Very well," said the troll-princess. "I shall take you to his room tonight."

She was as good as her word, leading the girl to the prince's chamber. But he was fast asleep and nothing the girl could do would wake him.

Next day she sat under the window again, with the golden carding comb in her lap. Again the troll-princess came to the window and again she made the same bargain with her. But the prince was fast asleep and though she wept and shouted and shook him, she couldn't get him to wake up.

The next morning the girl took her golden spinning-wheel and sat under the window till the troll-princess came. They struck the same bargain as the other times and the girl knew this was her last chance to see the prince.

But there were some other Christian folk in the palace captured by the trolls and they managed to tell the prince that a beautiful girl had come and wept over him the last two nights. The prince guessed that his bedtime drink was drugged, so that night he only pretended to drink it, and he only pretended to go to sleep.

When his chosen bride came to see him, he was awake and they fell into each other's arms. How proud he was of her for finding him and for her difficult journeys.

"But it is nearly too late," he said. "I must marry the troll-princess tomorrow. Still, I have had an idea. I'll say I want to wear the shirt you dropped the candle wax on and she must clean it for me. She won't be able to, because she is a troll and the wax was dropped there by a Christian woman."

Next day, the prince said, "I must see how fit my bride is to be my wife. Can you get the candle wax off my best shirt?"

The troll-princess tried but the more she washed it, the blacker the spots became, until the whole shirt was fouled and dirty.

"That is hopeless!" cried the prince. "Why, I bet that beggar girl over there could do a better job on it."

The "beggar girl" was his own true bride and as soon as she touched the shirt it became white as snow, white as the fur of the bear she had come to love.

"This is the girl I shall marry," said the prince.

And the troll-princess was so angry that she burst in

pieces with rage. And so did all the other trolls in the palace. The prince and his true bride released all the Christian prisoners and took all the silver and gold they could find. Then they left the palace that was East o' the Sun and West o' the Moon and never went back again.

Kate Crackernuts

Once there was a king and a queen who had each been married and each had a daughter. When they were unlucky enough to lose their wife and husband they each looked for someone else to marry. And as kings and queens don't have the same amount of choice as the rest of us, they picked each other.

They were married and were happy enough. The king's daughter was called Anne and the queen's was called Kate and the two girls became great friends. But the queen wasn't happy, because Anne was prettier than Kate.

So she plotted to see how she could take away Anne's good looks.

The queen went to see the hen-wife (who was also a witch) and told her the problem.

"Send the king's daughter to me tomorrow morning," said the old woman. "Only mind, she must have no breakfast before she comes."

"Anne, dear," said the queen sweetly, the next day. "Will you go to the hen-wife and see if she has any fresh eggs? Don't wait till after breakfast or all the best eggs will have been sold."

Anne obligingly skipped down to the village but, on the way, she picked up a crust from the freshly baked loaf cooling in the palace kitchen and munched it as she went.

When she reached the hen-wife's house, the old woman told her to lift the lid from a cauldron that was boiling on the fire and tell her what she saw there.

Anne thought this a strange place to look for eggs, but she did as she was told and saw nothing.

"Hm," said the hen-wife. "Haste ye back to the queen and tell her there are no eggs—and she should keep a lock on her pantry door!"

Anne didn't understand this either but she reported the message faithfully to the queen. Next morning, the queen sent Anne on the same errand, but this time she locked the kitchen door.

On the way to the village, Anne stopped to chat to some people who were harvesting peas. They gave her a handful of pods and she nibbled the sweet green young peas on her way to the hen-wife's cottage.

When Anne asked for the eggs, the same thing happened as the day before. The old woman told her to look in the pot and say what she saw, and Anne saw nothing. This time the message sent back was: "No eggs— and how do you expect the pot to boil when there's no fire?"

The queen understood the message a good deal better than poor Anne did and on the third morning she went with the girl to the hen-wife's house, making sure she ate nothing on the way.

This time, when Anne lifted the lid, her lovely head fell off and a sheep's head jumped out of the cauldron and settled on the girl's shoulders! Well, the queen had her wish now right enough, for her own daughter, Kate, was a good deal prettier than a sheep.

But Kate was furious when she heard what had happened. She took a fine silk scarf and wrapped it round her poor sister's head and both girls left the palace to seek their fortune.

They hadn't gone far when they

came to a fine castle. They knocked at the gate and were told that it belonged to a king who had two sons. One of the sons was very sick. He was tired out though he did nothing but lie in his bed all day. And the strange thing was that anyone who stayed up to watch the prince at night was never seen again, even though there was a fine reward of silver for anyone who could cure him.

"I'd like to try watching the prince," said Kate. "For my poor sister is sick, too, and I know what a sore trial it is."

So the king agreed to let the two girls stay, and that night Kate watched in the sick prince's bedroom. At midnight, the prince seemed to be sleeping, but he jumped out of bed and pulled on his boots and cloak and ran down the stairs to the stables. Kate ran lightly behind him and, when the prince whistled to his dog and saddled his horse, Kate jumped up behind him.

They rode out of the castle grounds and across country through the woods. And as they rode, Kate picked nuts off the trees and filled her apron with them. They came to a green hill with a door in it and the prince knocked.

"Who is it?" called a voice from inside.

"It is the prince, with his horse and his hound," said the young man.

"And his lady behind him," added Kate.

The door flew open and the prince rode in with his dog and Kate.

Inside was a magnificent fairy hall with feasting and dancing and music. Kate hid behind a pillar and watched while the prince danced and danced with the fairies till he was quite exhausted. Then they laid him down on a couch and fanned him till he was able to dance again.

When the cock crowed at daybreak, the prince left the fairy hall and rode back to the castle. In the morning, the king found the prince asleep in his bed and Kate sitting

by the fire, cracking nuts and eating them.

"He's had a good night, Your Majesty, but if you want me to watch another night, I'll need gold this time."

The king agreed and the next night everything happened as before. This time Kate saw a fairy baby playing with a wand in the corner. One of the older fairies said to another, "Just three taps of that wand and Kate's sister would be free of the sheep's head." Kate watched until no one was looking, then rolled some nuts towards the baby to play with. He dropped the wand and Kate immediately snatched it up.

At cockcrow, the prince rode back to the castle and Kate ran straight to Anne's room. She tapped her sister with the fairy wand and when Anne took the scarf off she had her own lovely face again. The sisters hugged and then Kate went back to the prince's room.

This time, when the king came in, Kate said she would stay up another night with the prince if she could marry him. The king agreed and on the third night everything happened as before. This time the baby was playing with a chicken and Kate heard a fairy say, "Three bites of that chicken would cure the prince." So she rolled some more nuts to the baby and was able to grab the chicken.

When the cock crowed, the prince rode back to the castle and Kate took the chicken to the kitchen. She plucked and roasted it and took it back to the prince's room. He woke to the smell of roast chicken and seemed to see Kate for the first time.

"That smells good," he said. "Can I have a bite?" When he had eaten the first bite, the prince sat up. Then he had

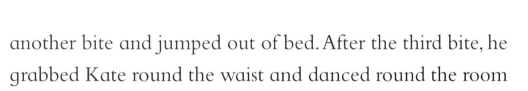

another bite and jumped out of bed. After the third bite, he grabbed Kate round the waist and danced round the room with her. Then they sat down and cracked nuts together.

The king came rushing in when he heard the commotion and so did Anne and the other prince.

"The prince is cured," said Kate, blushing, "and I claim my reward."

"A sack of silver, a sack of gold and my son for a husband!" said the king. Then he saw his other son making eyes at Anne and knew that there would soon be another wedding.

So the two sisters married their princes and all four of them were as happy as larks.

Dick Whittington

There was once a little boy called Dick Whittington who had a very poor start in life. He lived in a village in England, in the reign of King Edward the Third, where food was scarce. And it became even scarcer for Dick after both his parents died. The little boy was left an orphan and had to beg for food from the villagers.

He grew up a very hungry and skinny child, always dreaming of what it must be like to have a full stomach. Sometimes Dick heard people talk of London, the great city that was the capital of England then, as it is now.

The way they talked made it seem as if everyone in London was a rich lady or gentleman. "The streets are paved with gold there," they said. And that made Dick dream of a grand city with golden pavements where, if you were hungry, you could just break off a bit of gold and take it to the pastry-cook's to exchange for a meat pie.

He determined that the only way to make his fortune was to get to London. One day he saw a wagon, pulled by eight horses with bells on their harness, and he guessed it might be going to London. The wagoner was a kind man and took pity on the ragged boy who wanted to see the big city, so he gave him a lift.

Dick couldn't believe his eyes when he saw London. The buildings were so tall and grand, the streets were full of horses and carriages and there were people absolutely everywhere. Dick had never seen so many people all together.

"But where is the gold?" thought Dick. He searched everywhere, but the roads and pavements seemed made of dirt to him, not of precious gold.

He didn't know how to pay for food and his lodgings were the same dirty streets. He begged for a few pence, but Londoners weren't as kind to a poor ragged boy as the people in his own village, who knew him. So Dick went hungry.

He had nothing to eat for three days, and on the fourth he fainted on the doorstep of a rich merchant. Out of the house came the cook, who was very cross and not at all kind to beggars.

"Be off with you, you lazy lummox!" she shouted at Dick, "or I'll tip the dirty dish-water over you!"

At that moment, Alderman Fitzwarren, the merchant, arrived back at his house and he was a very kind man.

"What's all this?" he asked.

"Please, sir," said Dick. "I have had nothing to eat for a long time and all I ask is a bit of bread."

Mr Fitzwarren looked closely at him. "Why don't you work for your bread, boy?" he asked.

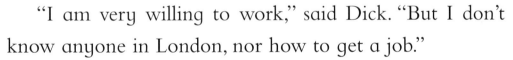

"I am very willing to work," said Dick. "But I don't know anyone in London, nor how to get a job."

"I'll give you a job," said kind Mr Fitzwarren.

And Dick was so pleased that he tried to jump up. But he was so weak that he just fell down.

So Mr Fitzwarren ordered Dick to be taken into the house, bathed in warm water, given warm clothes and fed till he was fit to work.

And when Dick felt strong enough, he was put to work in the kitchen helping the cook. Now, if it hadn't been for this cook, Dick would have been happy indeed. He always had enough to eat now and a roof over his head. And the Alderman's daughter, Alice Fitzwarren, was so pretty and always so nice to him that he might have thought he was in heaven.

But the cook made the kitchen seem anything but heaven. She was always scolding Dick and boxing his ears and threatening him with the ladle. "Idle boy!" she called him, and nothing he could do was right. The other problem he had was that his room up in the attic was full of holes and every night he was plagued by mice and rats running around it and even over his bed.

As soon as he had saved up a penny, he decided to buy a cat. So he got a lovely tabby cat, who was an excellent mouser, and she soon made short work of the mice and rats. Now Dick could sleep peacefully at night, but his days were still made a misery by the cook.

Now, Mr Fitzwarren was about to send one of his ships on a trading voyage, and it was his habit to let all his servants have the opportunity to send out something of their own to sell. He called them all to him and some sent a length of cloth or a waistcoat or even a lace handkerchief, whatever they could spare.

But poor Dick had nothing. Nothing, that is, but his cat. "I could send my cat," he told Mr Fitzwarren, and some of the servants laughed, especially the cook. But Mr Fitzwarren nodded seriously.

"I shall give her to the ship's captain and whatever he sells her for shall be yours."

So Dick was back with the mice and rats by night and the scolding cook by day. And as her temper got worse and his beatings more frequent, he decided he could bear it no longer. He set out back to the countryside early one morning. As day broke, he rested on a stone in a hilly, northern part of the city and looked back over its houses and churches. And at that moment the church bells began to ring and they seemed to say,

"Turn again, Whittington,

Three times Mayor of London!"

Dick was so astonished that he retraced his steps and went back to Mr Fitzwarren's house and put up with the cook and the mice and the rats.

Meanwhile, the merchant's ship had landed on the coast of Barbary, where the king and queen themselves were pleased to see its cargo. The captain was invited to dine with the royal couple and a splendid feast was set out before them. But before they could eat it, the room was overrun by rats who swarmed over the table and helped themselves to whatever they fancied.

The captain remembered Dick Whittington's cat. "I have something on board ship, Your Majesties," he said, "which could rid you of this plague."

And he went back to the ship and fetched the tabby

cat. As soon as she saw the rats, she struggled out of his arms and chased them, killing so many with her strong white teeth that there was soon a neat row of them laid out before the king and queen.

"What an amazing animal!" said the king, who had never seen a cat before. "Can we buy it off you?"

"I'm not sure, my dear," said the queen. "Would it not be too ferocious to keep in the palace?"

"Only to rats and mice, Ma'am," said the captain, lifting the cat and putting her on the queen's lap. The queen was very scared at first, but the cat, tired after her hunting, turned round three times, then curled up in a ball and started to purr.

The queen was then as delighted as the king and they bought all the ship's cargo for twice its proper worth and

then paid the captain the same sum
again for the miraculous cat.

When the captain arrived
at Mr Fitzwarren's house,
the merchant was very
pleased with his
profits. And he

was delighted with the news of Dick's good fortune. Some
of his household tried to persuade him to keep back some
of the money, since Dick was just a simple boy and
wouldn't understand.

But Mr Fitzwarren said, "No, he must have all that he
earned, for he gave up his cat, which was all he had."

And Dick was called from the kitchen and told he
needn't be a servant any more, since he was a rich man
now, all on account of his cat. As time went by, Dick had
new clothes and looked as handsome as any born
gentleman. He had a house of his own and soon asked
Alice Fitzwarren if she would share it as his wife. He
became Sir Richard Whittington and was Mayor of
London three times in his long and happy life. And all
because of a good old tabby cat.

Hansel and Gretel

Once upon a time a poor woodcutter and his second wife lived on the edge of a forest. The woodcutter's son, Hansel, and his daughter, Gretel, by his first wife, lived with them. They were very poor indeed and there came a day when they had no more food and no more money to buy any more food.

"Whatever are we to do, husband?" said the wife. "We cannot feed our children and we are all going to starve."

"I don't know," replied the wretched man. "I suppose we must keep on cutting wood and hope that things will get better."

"That's no good," said the wife. "We need a plan. I think we should take the children out into the forest with us, give them a last slice of bread each and then contrive to leave them, so that they are lost."

"But they will be devoured by wild beasts!" the woodcutter protested.

"Better that than for us to have to watch them starve. It will be a quicker death," said his wife.

And in the end, reluctantly, the woodcutter agreed with her. Now Hansel, who was a light sleeper, had heard all this conversation and went to tell his sister. She was horrified. "What can we do?" she cried.

"Don't worry, sister," said Hansel. "They may have a plan, but so do I."

And he went out into the moonlight and picked up handfuls of white pebbles from outside their hut.

In the morning, the whole family set off for the forest but, as they walked, Hansel kept stopping to leave a trail of white pebbles so that he and Gretel could find their way back. When his stepmother noticed that he was not keeping up, she asked

what he was doing and he replied, "I'm looking back because I can see my little white cat sitting on the roof as if to say goodbye to me."

"Foolish boy!" said his stepmother. "That is not your little white cat. It is the sunlight shining on the roof tiles."

The parents left their children, with a slice of bread each and a warm fire, in a glade in the forest, while they worked at cutting trees. But the woodcutter had fixed up a broken branch so that it knocked against a withered tree in the wind and sounded like his axe. By the time the children had discovered the trick, their parents were long gone.

But they ate their bread and waited till nightfall, when the moon came out. Then they followed the trail of white

pebbles back to their home. When they knocked at the door, their stepmother scolded them for getting lost, but their father was very pleased to see them.

And it happened that the food shortage eased and so the father was very glad that the plan to lose them in the forest had not succeeded. Time passed and there was another famine in the land. Again the woodcutter's family was reduced to their last half-loaf of bread and with no prospect of any more food.

So the woodcutter's wife suggested the same idea again. "Only this time we must take them further into the forest so that they cannot find their way back. This is the only way to save ourselves."

Secretly the woodcutter thought it would be better to share their last mouthfuls of food with their children and all starve together. But since he had said yes the time before, he didn't know how to say no this time, so in the end he agreed. But the children had overheard their parents talking and knew what was going to happen. Only this time the door was locked and Hansel could not collect any pebbles. "Don't worry," he told his sister. "I shall think of something."

In the morning, the parents gave each child a slice of bread, but Hansel crumbled his in his pocket and dropped the crumbs behind him as they walked. "What are you doing?" asked his stepmother sharply.

"I am looking at my little white pigeon on the roof that looks as if it is saying goodbye to me," said Hansel.

"Nonsense!" said his stepmother. "That is no pigeon. It is the morning sunlight shining on the chimney."

The parents took their children deeper into the forest than before and built them a fire. Then they went away to work, telling the children they would be back before dark. Of course, they never returned. At midday, Gretel shared her piece of bread with Hansel. And when it got dark and the moon came up, they tried to find their way home, but birds had come and eaten up all Hansel's crumbs, so they had no trail to follow.

"Now we are truly lost," wept Gretel.

"No, no," said Hansel, trying to keep her spirits up. "We'll soon find the way."

But they didn't. They walked all that night and all the next day, lying down to sleep in the leaves when they were tired, but they were still no nearer to finding their home.

By now they were very hungry, for there was nothing but a few berries to eat in the forest. They were lucky that they hadn't come across any wild beasts, because they would have been tasty morsels for a hungry bear or wolf.

Tired and hungry, they eventually stumbled into a clearing where there was a cosy little house. And when they got nearer to it, they could see that it was all made of food! The roof was made of gingerbread, the windows of spun sugar and the door and window sills of lovely sweet cake.

It was a long time since Hansel and Gretel had tasted anything sweet and they were very hungry, so they couldn't resist. Hansel reached up and broke off a piece of gingerbread roof. And Gretel, I'm sorry to say, began to lick one of the windows. How delicious it tasted!

But then the cottage door flew open and a very old woman came hobbling out on two sticks. The children were terrified but she seemed kindly enough.

"What charming children!" she said. "Who brought you here?"

Hansel and Gretel explained how they were lost in the forest and the old woman invited them in and gave them apple pancakes and glasses of milk. She didn't say anything about finding them eating her house.

When their stomachs were full, the children became

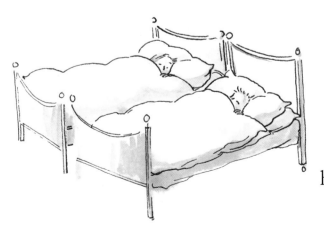

very sleepy and the old woman showed them to two little white beds. Hansel and Gretel thought themselves in heaven as they fell asleep. But they were wrong.

The old woman wasn't really sweet and kind. She was really a witch! She had it in mind to eat the two children and, in fact, her house was made of sweet goodies especially to entice children to her. She was a very wicked witch indeed.

In the morning, before the children were awake, she seized Hansel and locked him in a cage, because he was the plumper of the two. Then she shook Gretel awake and told her she must do all the housework and cook nice food for her brother, who was to be fattened up to be eaten.

Gretel was horrified, but she had to do what the witch told her. Now Hansel was fed chicken stew and sausages and gravy and dumplings and spotted dick with custard, while Gretel got only dry crackers and cheese rinds. Every day the witch reached into the cage to feel Hansel's finger, but her eyesight was so bad that he was able to deceive her by thrusting a chicken bone out.

"Why does he never get

any fatter?" grumbled the witch, as she felt the bone.

But after four weeks she was too impatient to wait any more.

"Boil up water on the stove," she told Gretel. "I'm going to cook that boy today."

Gretel wept and wailed but it was no good. She had to heat up the water.

"I'm going to bake some bread to have with him," said the witch. "I've made the dough. Now just creep into the oven for me and tell me if it's hot enough."

Now the wicked witch meant to shut the oven door on Gretel and bake her! But Gretel had her suspicions so she asked the witch, "What exactly do you mean? Would you mind showing me yourself?"

"Stupid girl!" muttered the witch. But she clambered into the oven and BANG! Gretel shut the door on her. And the wicked witch was burned to a cinder. Gretel rushed to get her keys from the rack and released Hansel from his cage. They embraced each other heartily, crying with relief over their escape from the witch.

Now they had nothing to fear so they explored the house and found chests of pearls and other precious jewels. Hansel stuffed his pockets with them, saying, "These are better than pebbles!" Gretel filled the pockets of her pinafore. She also helped herself to a nice piece of pie and a couple of apples but Hansel felt so full that he wasn't interested in food.

Their next thought was to get home, but they had no idea where they were. They started off in what they thought was the right direction. Before long they came to a broad stretch of water with no bridge in sight. But there was a white duck swimming on the water and Gretel asked her if she would take them across.

When they were both across, they walked a bit further and after a while their surroundings began to seem familiar. Then with joy they recognised the path to their old home. They rushed in through the door and found their father sitting very lonely in the downstairs room.

Their stepmother had died while they had been away and their father had missed his children terribly. He was so glad to see them again. And he was amazed when he saw all the pearls and jewels. From that day onwards they always had enough to eat. But Hansel never touched gingerbread again.

Rapunzel

There was once a couple who longed for a child and after a long time they were lucky enough to know that one was on the way. Then the wife had cravings for unusual food, as women expecting a child sometimes will. Nothing would satisfy her but some wild garlic from the garden next door.

The trouble was that this garden belonged to a witch. The woman's husband was very nervous about taking this plant from the witch's garden but his wife nagged and nagged him till he fetched some.

She greedily ate the plant, which was known in that

country as "rapunzel", and the man was very relieved. But a few days later, his wife was asking for more of this plant.

He brought her spring onions, but they wouldn't do.

"I must have the wild garlic, the rapunzel, or I shall surely die," she said.

So what was he to do? Twice more he crept back into the witch's garden. And the third time he was caught. The witch pounced on him and said, "Who is this who dares to steal from a witch's garden? Don't you know the penalty for that is instant death?"

The man fell on his knees and told her the whole story and begged for mercy. The witch thought about it, and said, "All right. You may keep the plant and your life. What is more, you can take all the rapunzel you need until your wife delivers her child. But the price of your life is that you must give me the child as soon as it is born."

The man was heartbroken at the thought of giving up the child he had longed for, and so was his wife when he told her what had happened. But they could do nothing about it.

A beautiful girl-child was born to them. They called

her Rapunzel, shed many tears over her, then
kissed her and handed her over to the witch.
Immediately the witch spirited the baby
away and brought her up in a tall tower
with no doors or stairways.

The baby grew up to be a most
beautiful young woman. Her finest
feature was her long shiny
hair, which she took great
care of. Every evening, the
witch would come to the
doorless tower and call,

"Rapunzel, Rapunzel, let down your gold hair,
And I will climb up it without a stair."

And Rapunzel would untie her long, long hair and let
it fall from her high window to the bottom of the tower,
and the witch would climb up it like a rope ladder.

Rapunzel had a very sweet singing voice and one
day, when she was singing in her tower room, a young
prince came riding by and fell in love with her voice.
He came closer to the tower and saw the beautiful
young woman at the window. But there seemed to be
no door and no way in to the tower.

As he watched, a hideous old woman hobbled up to the bottom of the tower and called,

"Rapunzel, Rapunzel, let down your
gold hair,
And I will climb up it without a stair."

Then the prince saw a cascade of golden hair fall from the window and watched as the witch climbed up it. Next day he came back to the tower and stood at the bottom and called softly,

"Rapunzel, Rapunzel, let down your
gold hair,
And I will climb up it without a stair."

When the torrent of golden hair spilled down around him, he wrapped himself in its thick coils and was soon in Rapunzel's room. She was very startled to see the prince, for she had never seen a man before, but he spent the whole day talking with her and by the end they were both in love.

The prince spent many more days with Rapunzel and asked her to marry him. He promised to bring a ladder so that Rapunzel

could escape with him. But the evening before, Rapunzel said innocently to the witch, "How is it that you are so much heavier than the prince? He never hurts my hair when he climbs up it."

The witch flew into a rage. "We'll soon put a stop to that!" she snapped, and she conjured up a huge pair of shining silver scissors and cut off Rapunzel's lovely golden hair. Then she spirited Rapunzel away to a far desert.

Back at the tower, the witch fixed the golden tresses to a nail in the wall and in the morning when she heard the prince calling,

"Rapunzel, Rapunzel, let down
your gold hair,
And I will climb up it without a stair,"

she let down the hair from the window.

Up climbed the prince. Imagine his horror when he found, not his beautiful bride-to-be, but an angry witch. The witch hissed at him, "Your songbird has gone and the nest is empty!"

In despair, the prince leapt down from the tower.

Luckily for him, he didn't break a leg, but he fell into some thorn bushes which pricked his eyes and he became blind.

He wandered the world for a long time until one day he found himself in a wild desert. Suddenly he heard a familiar voice, singing a sweet sad song.

"Rapunzel?" he cried. "Rapunzel, is that you?"

It was, and she came and saw her poor blinded prince and her heart was filled with love and pity for him and her tears overflowed and fell on his eyes. Miraculously he could see again and the first sight his eyes had was of Rapunzel's lovely face.

So they were married and lived happily together, and the prince didn't mind a bit that Rapunzel's lovely golden hair never grew any longer than to just below her pretty ears.

Thumbelina

Once upon a time there was a poor young woman who longed for a baby. So she went to a wise woman and said, "I do so want a baby, just a little tiny one. Can you help me?"

"Of course," said the old woman. "Take this magic barleycorn and plant it in a flowerpot. Water it carefully and see what grows."

So the young woman gave her a silver sixpence, took home the barleycorn and carefully planted and watered it. Suddenly, a large colourful flower burst forth, like a tulip, but with the petals tightly furled. The young woman was so pleased that she leant over and kissed the bud. Immediately, it opened its red and yellow petals and there, in the centre, was a tiny baby girl, no bigger than the woman's thumb.

"I shall call you Thumbelina," she cried, and was happy as can be.

The child had half a walnut shell for a cradle, violet petals for sheets and a rose leaf for her coverlet. She slept there by night and spent her days on the woman's table. Her mother had filled a plate with water and floated flower petals on it. Thumbelina sat on a tulip petal and spent the whole day rowing about, with two horse hairs for oars, on her own private lake.

One night, when Thumbelina was sleeping in her walnut shell, a large toad came hopping in through a broken window pane.

"That is just the wife for my son," said the toad, and took the whole cradle away in her mouth. She hopped out of the window and down to the muddy stream, where she lived with her son. As soon as he saw the little maiden, he said "Brekke-ke-kex, koax, koax!"—which was all that he could say.

"Don't wake her," said his mother. "Let's put her on a water lily pad. It will be like an island to her and she won't be able to escape."

How Thumbelina wept when she woke in the morning!

She had no idea where she was and there was nothing but water to be seen all around her. But she was even more alarmed when the toad and her ugly lumpy son swam up and told her she was to be married.

"We're just getting your bedchamber ready," said the old toad, and took her walnut-shell bed away.

Well, the fishes of the stream had heard the wedding plans and poked their heads out of the water to see the bride-to-be. And when they saw pretty little Thumbelina, they thought it would be a shame for her to have to marry the ugly toad. So they gnawed at the water lily stalk until it broke off, and Thumbelina went sailing down the river on her lily pad boat, far out of reach of the toads.

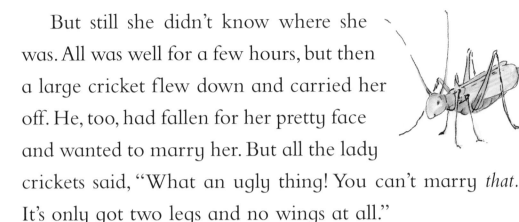

But still she didn't know where she
was. All was well for a few hours, but then
a large cricket flew down and carried her
off. He, too, had fallen for her pretty face
and wanted to marry her. But all the lady
crickets said, "What an ugly thing! You can't marry *that*.
It's only got two legs and no wings at all."

The cricket was sad, but he put Thumbelina gently
down on the ground. Now she was alone in a wood, where
she lived happily all summer, eating nectar from flowers
and drinking the dew and singing with the birds. There
was one swallow she was specially fond of, with his song
of "Quivit, quivit!"

But when autumn came and the days grew colder, there was nothing for her to eat, and the dew was turned to frost on the ground. Even the birds flew away. Thumbelina was so cold and hungry.

So she left the shelter of the wood and crossed the cornfield, which was all stubble by then, and came to a field mouse's house. There she knocked at the door and begged for some food. The field mouse was a kindly old thing and welcomed Thumbelina into her hole.

"You shall keep house for me and tell me stories," she said. "And in return you can eat all you want. I don't think a tiny thing like you will be a heavy burden on my larder."

So Thumbelina lived with the mouse and told her stories and sang her songs and was happy enough. Apart from one thing. The field mouse had a neighbour, Mole, and she was always singing his praises to Thumbelina.

"He has such a handsome black velvet suit, don't you think?" she would say. "He's very wealthy, you know. You would be a lucky girl if he asked you to marry him. Of course, being blind, he can't see how pretty you are, but you can charm him with your lovely voice."

But Thumbelina didn't want to charm him. She didn't like him at all. Mole hated the sunshine and flowers and life above the earth. He liked cold dark tunnels and worms and piles of dead leaves. But he liked Thumbelina, too, and was quite interested in marrying her.

One day Mole told the field mouse and Thumbelina that he had dug a new tunnel linking his home to theirs so that they might visit him more easily.

"Give it a try now," he said. "Only you mustn't mind, but there's a dead bird lying in it. Too much trouble to get him out."

So Thumbelina and the field mouse climbed the sloping tunnel to Mole's house. Halfway there, they came across the stiff bird, who was a swallow.

"Oh, poor swallow," cried Thumbelina. "You must have frozen to death. I wonder if you were the one who sang to me all summer?"

But the other two weren't at all sympathetic.

"See what all his squawking has brought him to," said Mole, who hated birds as much as flowers.

Later that night, Thumbelina crept back up the tunnel and laid a little blanket over the bird. She couldn't bear to think of him being cold. And next night, when she went to visit him, he opened an eye! He hadn't been dead at all, just fallen down in a frozen faint because of the bitter weather.

All winter long, Thumbelina brought him food and drink, and in the spring he was able to fly away in the warm sunshine. But with the spring came preparations for Thumbelina's marriage. Mole had proposed and she didn't know how to say no to him. The field mouse wanted it to

happen and she had been a kind friend to Thumbelina.

Now the mouse insisted that Thumbelina should sew all her own linen and clothes and get married in the autumn. The tiny girl made this job last as long as she could for she certainly was in no hurry to marry Mole.

But at last the fateful morning of her wedding came and she went out of the mouse's hole to bid farewell to the

sunshine. She wept to think that, once she was married to Mole, there would be no more sunny days for her.

Suddenly, there was a call of "Quivit, quivit!" and her old friend the swallow was there.

"Why are you crying, Thumbelina?" he asked.

"Because I am to marry the horrid old mole and live

under the earth for the rest of my days," she sobbed.

"Don't do that—come with me instead!" said the swallow. "The days are getting cold now and I must fly south for my sunshine. I missed it last year. Indeed, I should have died of cold if it hadn't been for you. Let me save you as you saved me."

"All right then, I will!" cried Thumbelina, drying her tears, and she climbed on the swallow's back.

He flew swiftly up and away, and soon the wood where Thumbelina had been left by the cricket was just a dot on the ground and she couldn't tell where the field mouse and Mole lived. She snuggled into the warmth of her friend's feathers and let him carry her south.

It was a long journey but well worth it. The swallow landed on a tree in a beautiful

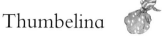

garden. The sun was shining with a full warmth that it had lost in the north, and brightly coloured flowers were in bloom.

"Where would you like to rest?" asked the swallow. "I have a nest in this tree, but it might be too high for you. Would you prefer a flower to sleep in?"

"Thank you, I think I should," said Thumbelina.

So the swallow swooped down to the ground with her.

And there, inside a red flower, she saw a tiny man, no bigger than herself! He wore a tiny gold crown on his head and had a pair of transparent wings. He was fast asleep, but woke up in some alarm when the swallow swooped down.

How he stared when he saw Thumbelina! He told her that he was king of the fairy people in that country and that

he had never seen anyone as lovely as she was. And Thumbelina thought she had never seen anyone as handsome as the fairy king. In fact, matters moved so fast that he soon asked her to be his queen. And since he was a much better match than a toad, cricket or mole, Thumbelina said yes.

The other fairies brought her her own pair of transparent wings and the couple were wed, with the swallow giving the bride away. And they all lived happily ever after.

Slow and Steady
Wins the Race

Stories with
a Moral

The Emperor's New Clothes

There was once an emperor who was very vain. He changed his clothes many times a day—indeed, he had a different suit for every hour. Every room in his palace had a full-length mirror, so that the emperor could check that his hat was on straight and that there were no wrinkles in his clothes.

One day, there came to his court two rogues who were weavers. They let it be known that they could weave a special cloth with this magical property: it could not be seen at all by anyone who was unfit for the job he held or was a simpleton.

The emperor soon got to hear of them and made up his mind to have a new suit of clothes made from this marvellous material. He gave the weavers lots of money and silk and gold thread (which they hid in their rucksacks). The two weavers set up their looms and very carefully pretended to weave the threads into cloth but, in fact, their looms were completely empty.

The emperor wondered how his cloth was coming along, but he didn't want to seem too eager, so he sent his oldest and most trusted minister in his place. The minister came into the weavers' room and watched them moving

their hands busily about their looms, but he couldn't see anything there.

"Oh, dear!" he thought. "Whatever can this mean? Surely I am not a simpleton? And as for being unfit for

my job, why, I have served the emperor faithfully for most of my life. What can I tell him about the cloth? I don't want him to know I can't see it."

"What's the matter?" asked one of the weavers. "Don't you like the design?"

"Look," said the other. "Can't you see the zigzags here and the twirly whirly bits there?"

"Of course, of course," said the flustered minister. "It's absolutely charming. I'm sure the emperor will be very pleased."

And he went back to the emperor and described all the zigzags and the twirly whirly bits with great enthusiasm. The next day, the emperor sent another ambassador to the weavers. He had the same problem: he couldn't see a thing. But he wasn't going to let on.

"How do you like the colour?" asked one weaver.

"Lovely, lovely," said the ambassador, clapping his hands and pretending to be very impressed.

"Do you think the purple goes well with the green and gold?" asked the other weaver.

"Quite enchanting," said the ambassador. "I'm sure

the emperor will love it."

And he went back to the emperor and described the purple and gold and green, not to mention the turquoise and orange. The emperor was very impressed. He couldn't wait to see for himself. So, the next day, he went to see the miraculous cloth. As soon as he entered the room, he felt very uncomfortable. Everyone was watching for his reaction. And he couldn't see a thing!

"What's this?" thought the emperor. "Am I a simpleton? Am I unfit to be emperor? We can't have everyone knowing. I must pretend I can see it."

So he praised the weavers for their work—"What fine design, what glorious colours!"—and ordered himself a suit to be made from the cloth. The weavers solemnly took his measurements and said the suit would be ready in the morning.

The emperor gave orders for a grand procession to be held the next day. He would walk through the streets of his city wearing his marvellous new suit, and all his subjects would look at him and be amazed. Word soon travelled through the city about the magic properties of the cloth, and the citizens got up early and lined the route of the procession.

The emperor got up early, too, and waited for the weavers. They had been up all night, with candles burning in their workroom. They pretended to pull the cloth off the loom, to cut it into shape and to sew it, with needles that had no thread in them.

In the morning, they came to the emperor's bed-chamber, which had more mirrors in it than any other room in the palace, carefully holding their arms out in front of them, as if they were carrying something.

"If Your Majesty would be so gracious as to take off your clothes," said one,

"we could fit you with your new suit."

"The material is so light," said the other, "that you won't even know you are wearing it."

Then they proceeded to put the imaginary suit on the emperor, adjusting the fit of the imaginary jacket, the fall of the imaginary cloak, buttoning the imaginary trousers and putting the imaginary hat into the emperor's hand.

"How do I look?" asked the emperor, twirling in front of the mirror.

"Magnificent", "handsome", "noble", "truly imperial", they all said.

And so the emperor set out on his procession. Six footmen in livery held a silken canopy over his head as he stepped out into the street. A gasp went up from the people. This is what they were supposed to see: a grand emperor clad in colourful and expensive clothes.

This is what they actually saw:

a rather plump middle-aged man wearing nothing at all.

But they all knew about the magic cloth and what it meant if you couldn't see it. So they clapped and cheered and threw their hats in the air and cried, "Long live the emperor!" and "Three cheers for our elegant and fashionable emperor!"

All except one little boy. He hadn't heard about the magic cloth. He tugged at his mother's sleeve and said in a very loud clear voice, "The emperor's got no clothes on!"

All of a sudden the crowd stopped cheering. The people looked at one another. Then they all started saying it. "The emperor's got no clothes on!", "The emperor's in his

birthday suit!", "Fancy walking down the street undressed!"
Even the courtiers started whispering to one another, and
the footmen holding the canopy just giggled, until they
could hardly hold the poles up. That was when the
emperor realised he had been tricked.

But there was nothing he could do except finish his
walk through the streets, as naked as the day he was born,
and then go back to the palace. The weavers were
nowhere to be seen. But, as soon as he got back, the
emperor put on his plainest, dullest suit. And he didn't
change it again all day. The very next morning he threw
out his full-length mirrors.

The Hare
and the Tortoise

The hare and the tortoise were having an argument over who could travel faster.

"It's obviously me," said the hare, appealing to all the other animals who were listening. "I mean, look at the size of my back legs! And I'm famous for my leaping and bounding through the fields."

"True, true," agreed the badger and the fox and the field mouse, nodding their heads.

The tortoise shrugged.

"We shall see," he said. "If you're so sure, you won't mind having a race with me."

"A race!" laughed the hare, running round the tortoise in circles. "What a crazy idea! I'm sure to win. But I don't mind making you look foolish. Name your time and place."

The animals settled on a race from the big oak tree in the hedge to the elm at the corner of the field, to be held at sunrise the next day.

Next morning, the tortoise was at the oak tree bright and early and,

as soon as the sun rose, he set off across the field at a steady pace. The hare, on the other hand, overslept. When he saw that the sun was already climbing high in the sky, he thought, "It will take the tortoise ages to get from one tree to the other. There's still plenty of time for me to overtake him."

And he yawned and went back to sleep. Meanwhile, the tortoise was plodding his way determinedly along the race course at about a quarter of a mile an hour.

By the time the hare woke up and got himself to the oak tree, he could see the dark hump of the tortoise's shell moving through the corn near the elm.

"Help!" thought the hare, and he put on all the speed he could with his big long back legs. But it was too late. As the hare reached the elm tree, panting with his efforts, the tortoise was already being congratulated by all the other animals on having won the race!

"But that's ridiculous!" gasped the hare. "Anyone can see I'm faster than he is!"

"Nevertheless," said the tortoise, calmly, "slow and steady wins the race."

And there was nothing the hare could do about it except go back to his den and sulk.

The Little Red Hen

Once upon a time a little red hen set up house with a cat, a dog and a pig. She was very hard working and did all the cooking and cleaning. The others were terribly lazy and didn't do anything they didn't have to.

One day, the little red hen thought it would be nice to have home-made bread. Her friends thought it was a good idea, too, so the little red hen started right at the beginning and bought some wheat.

"Now, who will help me plant the wheat?" she asked. The cat said, "I won't."

The dog said, "I won't."

The pig said, "I won't,
I won't, I won't."

"All right, then," said
the little red hen. "I'll just
have to do it myself." And she
planted all the wheat seeds herself.

Next she asked, "Who will help me water the wheat?"

The cat said, "I won't."

The dog said, "I won't."

The pig said, "I won't, I won't, I won't."

"All right, then," said the little red hen. "I'll just have to
do it myself." And she watered the
wheat every day.

Eventually it was
harvest-time, and
the little red hen
asked, "Who will help
me cut the wheat?"

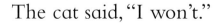

The cat said, "I won't."

The dog said, "I won't."

The pig said, "I won't, I won't, I won't."

"All right, then," said the little red hen. "I'll just have to do it myself." And she took a little scythe and harvested all the wheat.

Now it was time to grind the wheat to make flour. So the little red hen asked, "Who will help me take the sacks of wheat to the miller to be ground?"

The cat said, "I won't."

The dog said, "I won't."

The pig said, "I won't, I won't, I won't."

"All right, then," said the little red hen. "I'll just have to do it myself." And she got the farmer to take her to the miller's and back on his cart.

Now that she had the flour, the little red hen could make the first loaf.

"Who will help me make the bread?" she asked.

The cat said, "I won't."

The dog said, "I won't."

The pig said, "I won't, I won't, I won't."

"All right, then," said the little red hen. "I'll just have to do it myself." And she mixed the dough, kneaded it and left it to rise.

Some hours later, she asked, "Who will help me bake the bread?"

The cat said, "I won't."

The dog said, "I won't."

The pig said, "I won't, I won't, I won't."

"All right, then," said the little red hen. "I'll just have to do it myself." And she put the bread in the oven, watched over it to make sure it didn't burn, then took it out to cool when it was done.

A delicious smell of freshly baked bread filled the kitchen and the friends gathered round.

"Now," said the little red hen. "Who will help me eat the bread?"

The cat said, "I will!"

The dog said, "I will!"

The pig said, "I will, I will, I will!"

"All right, then," yawned the little red hen. "But you'll have to help yourselves. I'm going to sit down for a while. There's butter and strawberry jam in the larder."

And the little red hen sat down in the armchair and fell fast asleep. The three friends looked at one another and were ashamed. They knew they had done nothing towards making the bread.

The cat fetched a pillow and put it under the little red hen's head. The dog washed up all the cooking things. The pig made a big pot of tea for all of them and cut slices of the bread and spread it thickly with butter and jam.

When the little red hen woke up from her doze, she found the house clean and tidy and a tray on the table beside her with a mug of tea and a plate of bread and jam. She was very surprised.

"How kind you all are," she said. "You are the best friends in the world!"

And the cat, the dog and the pig all privately vowed that, from then on, they would be.

The Sun
and the Wind

The sun and the wind were always arguing about who was stronger and more powerful. One day, they decided to put it to the test. They saw a man walking along the road, who was wearing a fine new cloak.

"Whichever one of us can get that cloak off him," said the wind, "must be the more powerful, don't you think?"

"Definitely," said the sun. "You go first."

So the wind took a deep breath and puffed and blew until the poor man could scarcely stagger along the road. But the colder and windier it got, the more the man wrapped his warm cloak around him. The wind tugged at it and did his best to pull the cloak away, but the man clutched it ever harder.

"I think it's my turn, now," said the sun.

He shone with his most glorious beams on the man, who soon became quite warm. As he walked along the road, the hot sun made him sweat, so he unwrapped his cloak, unfastened it and, finally, he was feeling so warm that he had to take it off and sling it over his shoulder.

"Ha!" said the sun. "Who is the more powerful?" And the wind had to agree that the sun had succeeded where he had failed.

Which only goes to show that, if you want someone to do something, a warm smile can be more effective than bullying.

The Pigman
and the Princess

There was once a very handsome young prince who had not much money. But he had set his heart on marrying the daughter of the emperor who lived nearby. So he decided to send her the two most precious things he owned, as an engagement present.

One was a rose-tree that grew on his father's grave. It flowered only once every five years, and then had only one bloom at a time, but what a flower that was! It

was a perfect white rose with the most
heavenly scent in the world.

The other was a pet nightingale
which could sing any melody in the
world in perfect tune, so that it would
move anyone to tears who heard it.

The prince sent these two treasures,
with his messengers, to the emperor's
court, with a request for the
princess's hand in marriage. When they arrived, the princess
was very excited.

"Oh, what is in that packing-case, Papa?" she cried.
"Do you think it is a little pussy-cat?"

"No, my dear," said the emperor, as the
wrappings were removed. "It looks like
some kind of shrub."

"How prettily made that flower
is!" exclaimed one of the ladies-in-
waiting. The princess touched the
rose petals, then recoiled in disgust.

"It is not made at all!" she said,
horrified. "It is just an ordinary,
natural rose."

"Natural?" said the emperor. "What can the boy be thinking of?"

Then the messengers opened the other crate and there was the nightingale in his cage. As soon as he saw the light, he began his glorious song.

"It reminds me of that musical box the late empress had," said one of the old courtiers.

"But this nightingale isn't mechanical at all!" cried the princess. "It's an ordinary garden bird, whose cage will need cleaning like any other. I have no intention of marrying a prince who sends such cheap presents."

When the messengers gave the prince his answer, he was downcast for a while. Then he put on his oldest clothes, smeared his face with mud, and set out for the emperor's palace himself. He got himself a job feeding the emperor's pigs and bided his time.

He made a cunning little saucepan that was decorated with bells, which could play the tune, "Oh, my darling Clementine". It also had this magical property: if you put your finger in the steam from it, you could smell what was being cooked in every house in the kingdom.

One day, the princess was walking in the garden when she heard the bells playing:

"Oh, my darling, oh, my darling, oh, my darling Clementine!"

"I know that tune," she said. "I can play
it on the piano."

This was quite true, as the princess
could play only that one tune. Anyway,
she and her ladies-in-waiting drew
near to the pigsty to see where the
tune was coming from. And there
was the pigman, whose muddy
face couldn't conceal the fact
that he was very handsome.

"Ask him how much he wants
for the saucepan," said the princess.

"I shall accept ten kisses from the princess," said the
pigman.

"Out of the question!" said the princess, blushing
violently. But she wanted the little saucepan very much
and the pigman wouldn't change his price. So, in the end,
she told her waiting-women to crowd round her, so that no
one should see, and the pigman got his ten kisses.

Next, the pigman-prince made a rattle that could play
all manner of tunes, and everything happened as before.
The princess, walking in the garden, heard it and took her
waiting-women with her to the pigsty.

But this time the pigman wanted a hundred kisses!

"Not possible!" said the princess. "Tell him to take ten from me and the rest from you ladies-in-waiting."

But the pigman wouldn't have his kisses from anyone but the princess. So, at last, because she wanted the rattle so much, she got her ladies to cluster around and began to pay the price.

The emperor was looking out of his window and saw all the young women in the pigsty. Naturally, he was rather curious, so he went out of the palace in his slippers and crept up on them.

"What's all this?" the emperor said, loudly. And the

waiting-women sprang apart, revealing the princess giving the pigman his eighty-sixth kiss.

"Wretch!" shouted the emperor, and rushed in and boxed his daughter's ears. "Away with you both! I won't have a daughter who kisses a pigman; and I certainly won't have a pigman who kisses my daughter!"

Oh, what weeping and wailing there was from the princess and her women! But the pigman went to the pump in the yard and washed his face clean of mud. He got back to the princess just in time to hear her say, "How I wish I had married that prince who sent me the presents!"

"Madam, I am that

prince," said the pigman. "And I want to tell you that I despise you. You thought nothing of the scent of a real rose, preferring a magic saucepan which would let you smell potatoes and bacon cooking in the village. And you rejected my lovely living nightingale, though you were prepared to kiss a poor pigman to bits to gain an artificial music-maker. I am very glad that you are not going to be my wife."

And, with that, he left the palace and went back to his own kingdom, where we must hope he found a wife more to his liking. But, as to what happened to the princess, I do not know, so you can imagine whatever you think serves her right.

Belling the Cat

There was once a colony of mice living in an old house. Their lives were sweet and easy, with plenty to eat. But there was one cloud in their sky: the cat.

He was a huge fat ginger tom, but still very quick on his feet, and he liked nothing better than hunting mice. Almost every day, the mice lost one of their number to the swift paws and sharp teeth of the ginger cat.

The mice called a council to see what they could do. There was a lot of squeaking and muttering, but one mouse came up with an idea.

"If we were to get a bell and tie it round the cat's neck," he said, "we would always be able to hear when he was approaching. Then we could escape his clutches."

All the mice agreed that this was a really excellent idea. Indeed, they went so far as to get a bell and a ribbon. Now, all they needed was someone to volunteer for the job of tying it round the neck of old Ginger.

But, funnily enough, not one mouse came forward, not even the one who had suggested the bell. And to this day, for all I know, the big ginger cat is still catching mice, even though they know how to stop him, for want of a mouse brave enough to put the bell round his neck.

And it's no good our feeling superior to the timid mice, for how often do we humans also know the right thing to do, but don't do it because we are afraid? There is often not much to choose between us and those mice.

The Fisherman
and his Wife

There was once a fisherman and his wife who were so poor that they had to live in a pigsty. Every day, the fisherman went down to the seashore nearby, with his rod and line, and sat waiting for a fish to bite. If he was lucky, the couple had a fried fish supper; if he didn't catch anything, they went to bed hungry. And this was the pattern of their days.

One day, when he had been fishing for a long time with no success, the fisherman felt a bite on his line and he reeled in a huge flounder. But imagine his surprise when his fish started to talk!

"Please don't kill me," he cried. "I am not really a flounder, but a prince under an enchantment."

"All right," said the fisherman. "I wouldn't eat anything that talked, anyway." And he threw the flounder back in the sea.

When he arrived home empty-handed, his wife was very disappointed.

"Did you catch nothing at all, Husband?" she asked.

"Nothing but a magic flounder," said the fisherman. "He said he was really a prince, so I let him go."

"What?" said his wife, "and never asked him for any reward?"

"What should I have asked for?" said the fisherman.

"Oh, of course, we have everything we could wish for, living in a pigsty!" said his wife, angrily. "Go back down to the shore and ask for a little cottage for us."

So there was nothing for it but to go back to the sea. It was now all green and yellow and not as smooth as before. The fisherman stood on the shore and called:

"Flounder, flounder, in the sea,

Please come here and talk to me,

For my dear wife, Isabel,

Has a message I must tell."

Immediately, the fish came swimming up and said, "What does she want?"

"I'm sorry to bother you," said the fisherman, aware he was talking to a prince, "but my wife thinks I should have asked something in return for sparing your life. She would like a cottage."

"Go back," said the flounder. "She has it already."

So the fisherman went home and found his wife sitting on a bench outside a delightful little cottage, with a porch and a flower

garden and a yard full of ducks and chickens. And everything indoors was similarly charming, with farmhouse furniture and shining brass pans and green-and-white crockery.

The fisherman was very relieved, for it was a great improvement on the pigsty and the enchanted prince hadn't seemed to mind providing it. As they settled down to sleep after a good supper from their well-stocked larder, he said, "This is nice, Wife, isn't it? You must be happy now."

"We will see about that," said his wife.

And she was happy for a week or two, bustling about her new kitchen and making jams from the fruit in their little orchard. But after a while she began to think that, if the flounder could provide such a nice home for them, he could also provide one even grander.

"Go back to the flounder and ask him for a castle," she told her dismayed husband. "With servants."

The fisherman went back to the shore very reluctantly. The waves were purple and dark blue and grey. He called:

"Flounder, flounder, in the sea,

Please come here and talk to me,

For my dear wife, Isabel,

Has a message I must tell."

Along swam the fish. "What does she want now?" he asked.

"I'm afraid she'd like a castle, with servants," said the fisherman.

"Go back," said the fish. "You will find her in it."

So the fisherman went back home, and the cottage had vanished and in its place was a proper stone castle with a big flight of steps up to the door, and there was his wife at the top of them. She showed him round the grand rooms, which were a great deal too big for the fisherman's liking.

They were served their supper, and a very fine supper it was, at a long table waited on by servants in velvet livery, and the fisherman felt very uncomfortable. The couple went to bed in a large four-poster, with silk hangings and, as they settled down to sleep, the fisherman said, "Surely you are happy now, my love?"

"We will see about that," she said. And she began to think, what was the good of having a castle to live in if you were only a fisherman? Why not be king?

So, next morning, she told her husband to go back to the flounder and ask to be king.

"But I don't want to be king!" objected the fisherman. "I should dislike it very much."

"Then I shall be king," snapped his wife. "But you must go back and ask him."

The fisherman didn't want to go, but his wife gave him

no peace. So he went back to the shore, where the sea was now dark grey and rather smelly, and called:

> "Flounder, flounder, in the sea,
> Please come here and talk to me,
> For my dear wife, Isabel,
> Has a message I must tell."

The fish appeared immediately. "What now?" he asked.

The fisherman turned his hat in his hands, embarrassed. "Why, she wants to be king," he said at last.

"Go back," said the flounder. "She is king already."

When the fisherman returned to the castle, it was far larger than before, with extra towers guarded by soldiers with trumpets and drums. He could hardly find his way to the main hall, which was all decorated in gold. At the far end sat his wife, on a throne of diamonds. He could scarcely recognise her under her huge crown.

He approached the throne nervously. "Are you king now, Wife?" he asked.

"Yes, I am king."

"Then you are happy now, Wife? We shan't ask for anything more."

"No," said the woman. "I am not happy. If I can be king, then I might just as well be emperor. Go back and ask the fish."

"Nay, Wife," said the fisherman, very scared. "I can't ask that."

"You can and you will," said his wife, sternly. "Am I not your king? I command you to do it."

So there was nothing for it. The fisherman went back to the shore, dragging his feet. The sea was now thick and black and beginning to bubble like hot tar. He stood on the shore and called:

"Flounder, flounder, in the sea,
Please come here and talk to me,
For my dear wife, Isabel,
Has a message I must tell."

Along swam the fish. "What more does she want?" it asked.

"She wants to be emperor," said the fisherman, hanging his head.

"Go back," said the fish. "She is emperor already."

The fisherman thought he would never get into the palace which now stood where his home had been. Even the servants were dukes and earls, dressed in gold, and his wife sat on a throne of gold two miles high. The fisherman had to crane his neck to see her.

"Are you emperor now, then?" he called up to her.

"Yes, I am," said his wife.

"Then you are surely content, now?" asked the frightened fisherman. "For there is nothing greater left for you to be."

"Yes, there is," said his wife. "I want to be Pope."

"You can't be Pope!" said the fisherman, scandalised. "There is only ever one pope at a time, and you can't be it." He was sure that this was very wrong.

"If the flounder is powerful enough to make me emperor, he can make me Pope," said his wife. "Go, now, and ask him."

Very reluctantly, the fisherman turned and descended the long flight of marble steps. He walked as slowly to the sea as he could.

When he got there, the water was boiling and splashing on the shore, the sky was red and, on the horizon, two warships were firing guns at each other. The fisherman

trembled with fear, but called:

"Flounder, flounder, in the sea,
Please come here and talk to me,
For my dear wife, Isabel,
Has a message I must tell."

He was almost afraid to see the flounder, coming up out of the black water. "What on earth can she want now?" he asked.

"She . . . she . . . she . . . wants to be Pope!" the fisherman said.

"Go back," said the flounder. "She is Pope already."

The grand castle had vanished and in its place was a papal palace of the greatest splendour imaginable. At its centre was a cathedral, with doors thrown open to reveal its golden interior, rich with jewels and mosaics. Thousands of candles, some as tall as a house, lined the main aisle leading to a magnificent gold throne on which sat

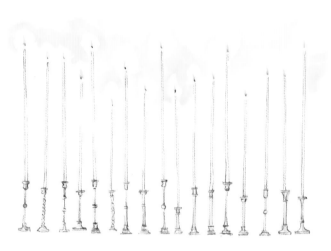

the fisherman's wife in her pope's robes. Kings and emperors queued up to kiss her feet.

When the fisherman could get near her, he whispered, "Wife, are you truly now Pope?"

"Yes," she said, stiffly.

"Then let that be enough," said the fisherman.

"We shall see about that," said his wife.

That night, she could not sleep. "There must be something more that I could have," she fretted. At last, she fell asleep, but was soon woken when the sun rose.

"That's it!" she thought. "If only I could tell the sun and moon when to rise and set!"

And she woke her poor husband and told him to go back to the flounder. "Tell him I must be able to rule the sun and moon—like God," she said.

"Like God?" said the fisherman. He was shaking all over, for he could see his wife was serious.

"Didn't you hear me?" said his wife, in a furious temper. "Go now this minute and ask the flounder to make me like God!"

And she kicked him down the stairs. The fisherman could scarcely make his way to the shore. There was a terrible storm raging. He had to stagger along the cliffs and down to the sea. The sky was pitch black and there was thunder and lightning. The waves rose as high as a church tower.

The fisherman stood on the shore in the wild wind and rain and called:

> "Flounder, flounder, in the sea,
>
> Please come here and talk to me,
>
> For my dear wife, Isabel,
>
> Has a message I must tell."

He couldn't hear his own words, but the flounder did and swam to him. "I can't believe there is anything more she could want," it said.

"You wouldn't think so, would you?" yelled the fisherman, over the wind. "But she wants to be like God!"

There was a huge clap of thunder, and then the storm stilled and the sea was like clear glass.

"Go back," said the flounder, "and you will find her in the pigsty, as before."

And there in the pigsty the fisherman and his wife are living to this day.

Mirror, Mirror,
on the Wall

Magical Stories

The Table, the Donkey and the Sack

There were once three sons who were driven out of their home by their father, because he thought they were lazy and careless fellows. But he was quite wrong, as you will see. The oldest son got himself apprenticed to a carpenter and learned his trade. When the time came for him to leave, the master carpenter gave him a little table. It was a roughly made object, nothing much to look at, but it had this magical property: if its owner set it on the floor and said, "spread yourself", the table instantly spread itself with a white cloth, laid with all the most delicious things to eat that you can imagine.

The young man was mighty pleased with this present and, wherever he travelled, never went hungry. Indeed, he often didn't bother to go to an inn but just set his table down by the side of the road and invited it to spread itself, and had as fine a dinner as he could wish.

One day, he found himself only a day's journey away from his old home. It was raining heavily, so he went to an inn, only to find it full of people.

"I'm sorry," said the innkeeper. "There are so many folk here, I doubt I'll be able to find you any supper."

"Never mind that," said the cheerful young man, "for I can find my own supper—yes, and some for all your guests, too."

And he set down his magic table and commanded it to spread itself.

Straightaway, it was covered with dishes giving off the most savoury and tempting smells. The other guests fell to eating and, as every dish was emptied, it filled itself up again, so that everyone was satisfied.

The innkeeper looked on in amazement. "That's a table worth having," he thought, and remembered that he

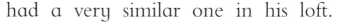

had a very similar one in his loft. When the young man had fallen asleep, propping his magic table against the wall, the innkeeper crept in and took it away, leaving the ordinary table in its place.

In the morning, the young man set off with the wrong table.

He had decided to go and visit his father, to see if they could be friends again. The tailor was very pleased to see him. "Son, tell me what you have done in all this time," he said.

"Well, Father," said the young man, "I have learned how to make furniture and I have this table."

The old man scratched his head. "I don't want to offend you, son, but that's not the best-made table I ever saw."

The young man laughed. "It's not of my making,

Father. It is a magic table
which will cover itself
with food whenever
I ask it. Let's have a
party for all our friends
and relations and
I'll show you."

So they invited
everyone they knew
and the young man put the
table down on the floor and said, "Spread yourself!"

Nothing happened.

Someone sniggered and the young man begged the
table again and again, but no food or drink appeared. The
tailor's dinner guests went home hungry and thirsty and he
felt very ashamed. But the son realised that he must have
been tricked and given another table.

Meanwhile, the second son had been apprenticed to a
miller. When his time was up and he knew his trade, the
master miller gave him a donkey. "Now, this is no ordinary
donkey," he said. "If ever you run short of money, just
spread a cloth under his tail and say the word 'bricklebrit'
and out of his bottom will come gold coins."

The young man couldn't believe his luck! He travelled the world, never lacking for money and, one day, found himself not far from his old home. He put the magic donkey in the stable of the very same inn where his brother had been cheated, and went in to see the innkeeper.

The innkeeper asked for two gold coins for a night's lodging and food and, when the young man took out his purse, he found that he had run out of money.

"Wait just a minute," he said, and went out to the stable, taking up a tablecloth on his way. Well, the landlord followed him in secret and watched as he spread out the tablecloth under the donkey's tail and said, "bricklebrit!" Out of the donkey's bottom came a shower of gold coins!

The innkeeper couldn't believe his eyes. And he decided to play the same trick as he had before. So the second brother left the inn with a perfectly ordinary donkey and went to see his father.

The tailor was delighted to have his second son back. "What have you been doing all this time?" he asked.

"I have learned the miller's trade, Father," said the young man, "and I have this donkey."

The tailor looked doubtful. "A cow would be more useful," he said. "What can you get from a donkey?"

"Well, from this donkey, which is a magic one, you get gold coins," said his son. "We are going to be rich, Father! Send for all our friends and relations and I'll fill their sacks with gold."

Well, after the disastrous dinner party, the tailor was very unsure, but he did as his son said and invited all their friends and relations to come bringing sacks. When they were all there, the young man spread a cloth under the donkey's tail and said, "Bricklebrit!"

What came out of the donkey's bottom was not gold.

The tailor was very embarrassed and all the people went home with empty sacks (except a cousin who had a vegetable garden and he was happy enough with the donkey's gift).

The youngest son had got himself apprenticed to a wood turner, who made the wiggly legs of grand tables and chairs. By the time he had finished learning, he had heard from his brothers about the cheating landlord who had stolen their magic gifts.

The master turner gave him a sack with a wooden club in it. "Whenever you are attacked," he said, "just say to the sack 'out of the sack, stick', and the club will leap out and beat your attacker."

That gave the young man a good idea, so he travelled straight to the inn where his brothers had been cheated. All evening he took good care of the sack, never letting it out of his sight.

"There are wonders indeed in this world," he told the people there. "I have heard tell of tables that spread themselves with food and donkeys that can poo gold, but there's never been anything like this sack."

The innkeeper listened carefully and was sure that the sack must be filled with precious jewels or something. At nightfall the young man went to bed with the sack under his head and pretended to fall asleep. In crept the landlord

with an old sack filled with empty beer bottles, and began to tug at a corner of the young man's sack.

Immediately, the young man leapt up and said, "Out of the sack, stick!" and out jumped a wooden club that beat the landlord till he cried for mercy!

"Not until you give me back my brothers' table and

donkey," said the young man. So he got back the magic gifts and travelled home to his father's house. The old tailor was very pleased to have him back. And so were his brothers, especially when they saw what he had brought with him. They had the feast after all and this time all their friends and relations went home with full stomachs and full sacks of gold, too.

And the tailor and his three sons lived well and happily ever after, never wanting for anything. And no one ever tried to rob them again, for word of the stick in the sack soon got around.

Sleeping Beauty

There was once a king and queen who longed to have a child. They waited many years but, at last, the queen gave birth to a beautiful baby girl. How proud the king was of his little daughter! He wanted her christening party to be the grandest ever seen.

He invited all their friends and relations from far and wide and also invited the fairies who lived in the kingdom. He thought that they might give the little princess special gifts. But there were thirteen fairies in the land and the king had only twelve sets of special gold plates and cups and knives and forks. He had to leave one fairy off his invitation list, so he chose the grumpiest and most unkind.

When the day came, there was a splendid feast and everyone had a very grand place setting, but none so grand as the golden ones set before the twelve fairies. After the feast, the fairies started to give their magic gifts to the princess.

One gave beauty, one kindness, one wealth, one a lovely singing voice and so on, until eleven fairies had bestowed their blessings and the princess was a very lucky baby indeed. But then, disaster! The thirteenth fairy, the

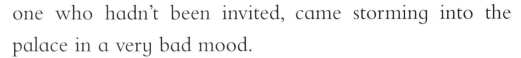

one who hadn't been invited, came storming into the palace in a very bad mood.

"This is my gift," she said. "When the princess is fifteen years old, she will prick her finger and fall down dead!" Then she gathered up her skirts and flounced out without another word.

Everyone was appalled by what had happened, but the twelfth fairy, who hadn't yet given her gift, said, "I cannot completely change the last wish, but I can soften it. She shall not die, but shall sleep for a hundred years, she and the whole court."

After that, the party cheered up, because the princess was not doomed to die after all and fifteen years seemed a long time. All the same, the king issued a decree that all needles, pins and spindles should be banished from the kingdom, which meant that all sewing and spinning had to be done outside its borders, which was very inconvenient.

All the good gifts that the fairies had given the princess at the christening made her life pleasant. She was so lovely to look at that everyone loved her and she had a sweet nature to go with it. She sang like a nightingale, danced like a leaf in the wind and could play several musical instruments, as well as being able to paint and draw and write elegant verses.

She had a golden childhood but, on her fifteenth birthday, when her parents were busy arranging her party, she went exploring in the palace and came across a staircase she had never seen before. She climbed the winding stairs and came to a little room, where an old woman sat working at a spinning-wheel.

"Good day, mother," said the princess, politely. "What are you doing?" Remember, she had never seen a spinning-wheel, for all spindles were banned from the kingdom.

"Why, I am spinning, child," said the old woman, who was really the bad fairy in disguise.

"And what is that, which spins round so merrily?" asked the princess, and she touched the spindle. Immediately, it pricked her finger and she fell down onto the bed in that room, in a deep sleep.

The king and queen also fell asleep, and so did all the courtiers and servants. The horses went to sleep in their stables, the dogs in the yard, the pigeons on the roof. Even the fire blazing in the grate was frozen in stillness.

And so they all stayed for a hundred years and no one grew any older. But round the castle sprang up a huge hedge of rose-bushes with long thorns, so dense and tough that no one could get through it. And over the years many young men tried. For it was rumoured that a beautiful girl lay sleeping behind it.

But, as the years went past, it seemed more and more like an old legend and no one remembered any of the people who lived in the palace. Then, one day, a king's son came riding by. He had heard the legend of the Sleeping Beauty and meant to see if he could find her. He was very lucky, for the hundred years were nearly up and the hedge had lost its thorns. He pushed his way between the sweet-smelling roses and found himself in the courtyard where all the dogs lay asleep.

There was not a sound from the stables, except the gentle snoring of horses and up on the roof all the pigeons had their heads under their wings. The prince entered the hall and saw the king and queen, sleeping where they had collapsed on their thrones. In all the palace not a soul was awake.

The prince explored the whole palace and eventually

found the winding stair with the little room at the top. The bad fairy and the spinning-wheel had gone, but there on the bed lay the sleeping princess. The prince thought she was the most beautiful person he had ever seen. He couldn't resist; he just leaned over the bed and kissed her.

At that moment, the hundred years of the spell were over. The Sleeping Beauty woke up and smiled at the prince. He took her hand and led her downstairs to the hall, where her father and mother were waking up, too.

The fire started to burn in the kitchen grate, the meat began to roast again and there was soon food enough for a banquet. The prince and princess were married shortly afterwards and lived happily ever after.

Snow White

Once upon a time a beautiful queen sat sewing at her window. It was winter and her ebony window framed a landscape all white with snow. The queen pricked her finger and, as the bright blood welled up, she thought, "How I wish I had a little girl whose skin was as white as snow, whose hair was as black as ebony and whose lips were as red as this blood!"

And, by the end of the year, the queen's wish came true, for she gave birth to a baby girl, whose skin was as white as snow, her hair black as ebony and her lips red as blood.

But it was a hard birth and the queen died of it. The king was very sad and he called his little daughter Snow White.

Time went by and the king was lonely, so he married again. His second wife was a beauty, too, but a very vain one. She had a magic mirror in her bedchamber and every morning she spoke to it:

"Mirror, mirror, on the wall,
Who is the fairest one of all?"

And the mirror would reply:

"The loveliest creature ever seen
Is none but you, O gracious queen!"

The queen was not fond of Snow White, who grew prettier with every day. So imagine her shock when, one day, she asked her mirror, "Who is the fairest one of all?" and heard this reply:

"She who makes the darkness bright,
The lovely princess called Snow White."

The queen was furious, but she knew that the mirror never lied. So she made a terrible plan. She called the palace's chief huntsman to her and told him to take the child into the forest and kill her.

"And when you've done it, bring me her lungs and liver as proof!" said the wicked queen.

The huntsman went to call Snow White to join him for a walk in the forest. She went with him happily because she knew all the people who worked in the palace and they were all nice to her. As they got deeper among the trees, the huntsman thought he really couldn't kill the sweet, pretty girl. So he told her about the queen's orders. "Run away, Snow White," he said, "and God keep you safe."

But he secretly thought she would probably be killed by wild beasts anyway.

As he travelled back to the palace, the huntsman killed a wild boar and took its lungs and liver to the queen.

"So, it is done," she said. "Tell the cook I'll have them for supper."

Snow White was very scared alone in the forest. But no animals harmed her and, in the end, she came to a little cottage with smoke coming out of the chimney, which looked cheerful and welcoming.

There was no one at home, but Snow White had to rest, so she went in. There was a wooden table set with seven little plates, seven little mugs and seven little knives and forks. There was food on the plates and wine in the mugs and Snow White was so hungry that she took a little bread and vegetable from each plate and a sip of wine from each mug, so that it wouldn't be missed all at once.

Then she saw seven little beds lined up against the wall. She was so tired that she wanted to go to sleep in one of them, but one was too short, one too soft and one too lumpy. She tried them all and the seventh one seemed the most comfortable, so she snuggled under the covers and fell fast asleep.

When it grew dark, the owners of the house came

home. They were seven dwarves, who worked in the mines all day, digging out copper and gold. As soon as they got inside they knew someone had touched their meal and they could see dents in their beds. But the seventh dwarf found a little girl fast asleep in his!

The dwarves gathered round to admire the sleeping child. They were kindly creatures and thought they had never seen anything so lovely as Snow White. At that moment, she woke up and saw seven little faces with white beards, looking down at her. She told them her story, about how her stepmother had wanted to kill her and how she had run away.

"That's all right, my dear," said the dwarves. "You'll be safe with us, as long as you don't let anyone into the house. You can stay here and we'll look after you but, in

return, you must do all the cooking and
cleaning and tidying of the house."

"I'd like that," said Snow
White.

When they had eaten
their supper, they went to
bed and the seventh dwarf
slept one hour in each of the
other dwarves' beds so that
Snow White could have his.

Back at the palace the next morning, the queen asked
her mirror:

"Mirror, mirror, on the wall,
  Who is the fairest one of all?"

But the mirror replied:

"O Queen, you are fairest of all I see,
  But over the hills, where the seven dwarves dwell,
  Snow White is still alive and well,
  And none is as fair as she."

Then the queen knew she had been tricked and plotted
even harder to get rid of Snow White. She disguised herself

as a pedlar-woman and went to the dwarves' cottage.

Snow White was happily dusting and sweeping while the dwarves were at the mines, when she heard a voice calling, "See my lovely ribbons and laces. Pretty things for pretty girls." Snow White couldn't resist and she opened the door. The pedlar-woman stepped in and said, "Wouldn't you like to buy yourself something nice as a treat after all your housework? How about this lace?"

And she showed Snow White a rainbow-coloured lace for her bodice. "Here, let me thread it for you," said the old woman, and she laced Snow White so tightly into her bodice that she couldn't breathe and fell down on the floor.

When the dwarves came home they thought their little friend was dead. But they quickly cut the rainbow lace and Snow White could breathe again. She told them what had happened. "But that must have been the wicked queen," they said. "You must be on your guard and not let anyone in the house."

Back at the palace, the queen asked the mirror her usual

question. But the answer came:

"While Snow White breathes and shows her worth,
    She's still the fairest on this earth."

The queen ground her teeth with rage and thought how she might kill her enemy. She knew all sorts of witchcraft and disguised herself again to look like a quite different old woman. Then she put poison on a hair comb and set out for the dwarves' cottage.

Snow White was baking an apple pie when she heard a voice saying, "Who would like something pretty for her hair?" Snow White opened the door and saw an old woman with a tray full of bows and slides and pretty combs.

"I know just the thing for you," said the old woman, holding out the poisoned comb. "Just think how these sparkling stones will set off your dark hair."

And Snow White was so fond of sparkly things that she let the pedlar in. The old woman showed her the comb and put it in her hair. Immediately, the poison entered Snow White's skin and she fell down in a swoon. But luckily it was nearly time for the dwarves to come home and, as soon as they found her, they drew the comb out of her hair.

Snow White sat up, well as ever and anxious to get her pie in the oven. But the dwarves were very worried. "You really must promise not to open the door to anyone," they told her. "The queen is determined to kill you."

Back at the palace, the queen spoke to her mirror and it said:

"The loveliest creature alive tonight
　Is the beautiful princess called Snow White."

The queen tore her hair with fury. She used all her witchcraft to make a poisoned apple. It was red on one side and white on the other and looked as tasty as an apple can be, but one bite from the red side was deadly.

Then the queen turned herself into a farmer's wife and went to the dwarves' cottage.

Snow White was making a pair of curtains when she heard a voice call, "Apples, apples, nice sweet apples!" Now, Snow White was

very fond of apples, but
she knew she mustn't open
the door. So she opened
the window instead. How
delicious the apple looked
that the farmer's wife was
holding out to her!

"Apple, my pretty?" asked the old woman.

Snow White shook her black hair. "I'm not allowed,"
she said.

"Whyever not?" said the old woman. "They're good
and wholesome. Look, I'll take a bite myself." And she bit
out some juicy flesh from the white side of the apple. Then
she held out the red side to Snow White. The little girl
couldn't help herself. She took a bite.

Immediately, Snow White fell down dead and the
witch queen ran happily back to the palace. When the
dwarves came home, they could not revive Snow White.
They looked for laces and combs but didn't think to look
inside her mouth. Sadly, they agreed that she must be
dead, but she still looked so beautiful that they couldn't
bear to bury her. So they made a glass coffin and put
Snow White in it, and put it on a hilltop nearby. One of

the dwarves watched over the coffin every day.

The queen was happy at last in her palace, for whenever she asked the mirror,

"Mirror, mirror, on the wall,
Who is the fairest one of all?"

it replied:

"The loveliest creature ever seen
Is none but you, O gracious queen."

And she was very happy that her rival was dead at last.

As for the dwarves, they missed Snow White very much. She didn't change a bit, keeping her rosy cheeks and her white complexion. Years went by and, one day, a young king was out hunting in the hills. He saw the glass coffin and immediately fell in love with the beautiful girl who seemed to be sleeping in it. He spoke to the dwarf who was on guard by the coffin and heard the whole of Snow White's story.

The king begged and pleaded with the dwarves to let him take the glass coffin back to his kingdom, so that he could continue to gaze at the girl. He offered them a large heap of gold in return. At first they wouldn't hear of it, but he seemed so broken-hearted that eventually they said yes.

The king had the coffin put on a carriage pulled by horses but as they set off through the forest, the first horse stumbled on a tree root. The coffin slipped off and fell on the ground, tipping Snow White out. And, with that, the piece of poisoned apple was dislodged from her mouth. She woke and found herself looking into the eyes of a handsome young man.

In a moment the king was on his knees asking Snow White to marry him, and she was happy to say yes. She said goodbye to the seven dwarves and went to live with her king in his kingdom. The invitations soon went out to a grand wedding.

Now, when Snow White's wicked stepmother got her invitation, she spent days getting herself ready. When she was dressed in all her finery, the wicked queen asked her mirror:

"Mirror, mirror, on the wall,
   Who is the fairest one of all?"

and got this reply:

"Of all ladies here you the loveliest are,
   But the new young queen is fairer by far."

The queen turned pale with fury. But she was even more furious when she arrived at the wedding and saw that the bride was Snow White! She was so angry that she couldn't move. All her magic froze up inside her and she turned to stone. Snow White lived happily with her king and she had the wicked queen moved to the park where she made a beautiful statue for the birds to sit on.

The Three Heads
in the Well

Long ago in England, well before the time of good King Arthur and his knights, there reigned a king in Colchester. He had a lovely queen who died, leaving him the care of their fifteen-year-old daughter. The king was a bit short of money, so he married a rich widow who was very ugly and who had a daughter as unattractive as herself.

Now, the new queen was jealous of the king's pretty daughter and planned to turn him against her. She made up lots of horrid stories about the princess, and she was so successful that the king believed her and told his daughter that she must leave home and go to seek her own fortune in the world.

So off she was sent, with nothing but a canvas sack with some brown bread and hard cheese in it, and a bottle of beer. The young princess said thank you for the food and then travelled along the road till she came to a cave, with an old man sitting outside it.

"Where are you going, pretty maid?" he asked.

"To seek my fortune," said the princess.

"And what is in your bag and bottle?"

"Just bread and cheese and beer," said the princess, "but you are welcome to share it."

So they divided the little picnic and the princess kept her half for later. When the old man had finished eating, he gave the princess a wand and said, "You will soon come to a thorny hedge, but just tap it with this wand and you will pass through safely. Then you will see a well with three golden heads in it. Do whatever they ask you, and you will be rewarded."

The princess thanked him and went on her way. She came to the high thorny hedge and tapped it with the wand. Straightaway,

the hedge parted and she could walk through without a scratch. On the other side was a well.

When the princess approached it, up bobbed a golden head, singing this song:

"Wash me and comb me
And lay me down gently,
Put me on the bank to dry
So I may look pretty
To those who pass by."

The princess was very surprised, but she lifted the head gently out of the well and washed its face carefully and combed its tangled hair with a little silver comb she had brought in her pocket. Then she laid the head down on the grass to dry.

Two more heads popped up, one at a time and sang the same little song. Twice more the princess washed and combed them and, when all three heads lay on the grass, she sat down and ate her lunch.

The three heads talked to one another:

"What shall we give this girl who has been so kind to us?"

The first one said,
"She shall stay as beautiful
as she is today and win the
heart of a great prince."

The second one said,
"She shall have a voice
as sweet as a nightingale's."

And the third said, "She is
the daughter of a king and shall
be a greater ruler than he."

When the princess had finished her food, she said goodbye to the golden heads and went on her way.

Before long,
she met a handsome
young king out riding with his dogs. He fell in love with
her beautiful face and kind ways and they were soon
married.

The young king discovered that his beautiful wife was
the daughter of the King of Colchester and said that they
must go and visit him. Imagine how surprised the old king
was to see his daughter coming back dressed in silks and
lace and wearing expensive jewels!

Her husband told his father-in-law all about the heads
in the well and the ugly queen overheard him. "It's not fair
how well that girl has done for herself!" she protested. "My
daughter must have the same chances."

So she sent for her own daughter and gave her a velvet

bag with roast chicken and sugared almonds and a bottle of sweet wine and sent her out on the same road the other princess had taken.

But this was a very different sort of girl. When she met the old man at the cave, he said, "Where are you going, young woman?" and she replied, "Mind your own business!"

"What have you in your bag and bottle?" asked the old man.

"All manner of good things," said the rude girl, "but you're not getting any."

When she came to the thorny hedge, the girl saw a gap she thought she could climb through. But, as soon as she tried to pass, the hedge closed up and pricked her skin with a thousand thorns.

Once she was through, the girl was bleeding from all her scratches and in a very bad mood, as you may imagine. She flounced over to the well to clean off the blood and saw a golden head sitting in it.

> "Wash me and comb me
> And lay me down gently,
> Put me on the bank to dry
> So I may look pretty
> To those who pass by."

sang the head.

"Take that!" said the girl and banged the head with her bottle. The two other heads fared no better. The grumpy girl sat on the grass and ate her delicious lunch. Meanwhile, the heads asked one another, "What shall we do for this horrible girl?"

The first one said, "I'll curse her face with an ugly rash."

The second one said, "I wish her a voice as harsh as a corncrake's."

And the third one said, "I wish her a poor country cobbler for a husband."

When the girl had finished her lunch, she went on her way and reached a village. All the villagers ran screaming when they saw her face all covered with spots and heard her harsh voice. The only person who stayed was the cobbler.

He had recently mended some shoes for a poor hermit, who had paid him with a special ointment to cure skin rashes and a potion to cure a harsh voice. He felt sorry for the girl and asked her who she was.

"I am the King of Colchester's stepdaughter," she said, though by now she wasn't quite as proud as before.

"Then, if I heal your face and your voice," said the cobbler, "will you marry me?"

The girl had been so upset when everyone ran away from her that she said yes.

So she married the cobbler and they went to visit the court at Colchester. The girl's mother was so disgusted that she had married a cobbler that she refused to talk to her, but the king was highly amused. He paid the cobbler a hundred pounds.

So the ugly girl and the cobbler lived together quite comfortably and, if they weren't quite as happy as the pretty girl and her king, they weren't much less so, for the girl had learned her lesson and was a much nicer person than when she met the three heads in the well.

Rumpelstiltskin

Once upon a time there was a poor miller who found himself called to do business with a king. You might have thought that would be enough for him, but no, he had to start boasting, so that the king would think he was someone important.

"I have a daughter," he said, which was true enough. "And she is remarkably beautiful," he said, which was also true. But then he added, "And she has this gift, that she can spin straw into gold."

Oh, foolish miller! Why didn't he stop after saying he

had a beautiful daughter? For no one can spin straw into gold and he was just asking for trouble.

"Really?" said the king, raising his eyebrows and looking at the miller's dusty apron. "That is a very useful gift indeed. Bring her to me so that she may show off this skill."

Now the miller was well and truly in the soup. He wished he had kept his mouth shut, but it was too late for that. He had to bring his daughter to the palace. The king showed her into a large room full of straw, with a spinning-wheel in the middle.

"Here you are, my dear," he said, kindly. "As much straw as you like. Turn it all into gold by morning or you must die."

The poor girl didn't know what to do. She hadn't the faintest idea how to start turning straw into gold, any more than you or I do. So she sat on a bale of straw and wept.

Suddenly a funny little man appeared and asked her what was the matter.

"I have to turn all this straw into gold by morning," sobbed the girl, "or I shall die."

"Well, that's nothing to cry about," said the little man. "I can do that. But what will you give me if I do?"

The miller's daughter said she would give him her necklace and the little man agreed. The girl curled up on the straw and slept peacefully all night to the hum of the spinning-wheel, until the little man needed the bale she was lying on, because he had filled every reel with spun gold.

By dawn the little man had disappeared and the room was full of reels of gold. The king couldn't believe his eyes and the miller's daughter was mightily relieved. But, that evening, the king took her to an even bigger room with even more straw in it and gave her a spinning-wheel.

"You did so well yesterday," he said, smiling. "I'm sure you will manage to turn this lot of straw into gold, too."

The girl wasn't sure at all, until the little man appeared again. He looked at all the straw.

"What will you give me this time?" he asked.

"The ring from my finger," said the girl, taking it off. And, though it was of no great value, the little man took it and set to work. By morning the room was full of spun gold.

And was the king content? You can probably guess by now what he did. He took the miller's daughter into a barn, filled with straw from floor to ceiling, so that there was scarcely room for the spinning-wheel to be squeezed in.

"This is the last time I shall ask you, my dear," said the king. "But if you turn all this straw into gold, I shall make you my queen." (For the miller's daughter really was very pretty.) "But," added the king, "if you do not, I'm afraid the terms are as before and you will die."

The girl sat at the spinning-wheel and wept. It didn't even cheer her up to see the little man appear, for she knew she had nothing left to give him.

"What, nothing?" he asked, when she explained the situation.

"Nothing at all," she said.

"All right," said the little man. "I will do it for you, but you must promise me that, if you ever become queen, you will give me your first-born child."

So the girl promised; what else could she do? And by morning the whole barn was filled with spun gold. The king clasped her in his arms and kissed her and she was queen within a week.

It had all happened so suddenly that it seemed like a dream and she forgot all about her promise. A year after the marriage, the young queen gave birth to a healthy baby boy. She was delighted with him, like any new mother. But while she was cooing over her pretty baby, the funny little man suddenly appeared in the royal bedroom and reminded her of her promise.

She was horrified. "You can't mean it!" she cried, clutching her

precious baby son. "I shall never give him up.
Think of something else."

And she offered him all the riches of her
husband's kingdom—jewels,
gold, carriages, houses.
But the little man tapped
his foot impatiently.

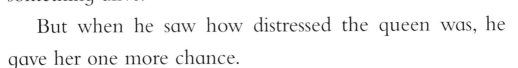

"What do I want with
all that stuff? You know
I can turn even straw
into gold. I want
something alive."

But when he saw how distressed the queen was, he
gave her one more chance.

"I'll give you three days to guess my name. If you
can't, then the child is mine." Then he vanished. The next
day he was back and the queen began, "Is your name
Caspar? Melchior? Balthasar . . . ?" and she worked her
way through all the names in the Bible. But, by the end of
the day, the little man had said no to every one.

On the second day, she tried all the weird names she
could think of, like Shortshanks and Grungefoot and
Lumpybottom. The little man became more and more

insulted, but the queen still hadn't discovered his real name.

That night she was in despair as she rocked her baby boy. She thought she would never guess the little man's name in time. Then she heard two of her servants talking. One had been out in the forest and had come to a hut with a fire outside it.

"And dancing round the fire was a funny little man singing a song," said the servant. "It went like this:

'Today I'll brew, tomorrow bake,
Then have the princeling, no mistake.
I need no fortune nor no fame,
RUMPELSTILTSKIN is my name!'"

The queen was so excited. Next day, when the little man came, she asked, "Is your name Leonardo?"

"No," said the little man.

"Is your name Brad?"

"No, no," said the little man. "You'll never get it!"

"Then," asked the queen, "is your name . . . Rumpelstiltskin?"

"Who told you, who told you?" screamed the little man, stamping his foot on the floor in such a rage that it went right through the floorboards. He pulled at his leg so hard that he split himself in half, and that was the end of Rumpelstiltskin.

The Twelve Dancing Princesses

O nce upon a time there was a king who had twelve daughters and they were all great beauties. He was very fond of them and didn't want them to leave him and find husbands, so he took great care that they shouldn't go out to parties and meet young men.

The twelve princesses all slept in one large bedroom and, every night, the king locked the door to it himself, to make sure they didn't creep out after dark. But here was a mystery. Every morning the princesses' shoes were worn to shreds, as if they had been dancing all night!

They wouldn't tell their father how this came about, and he was quite distracted. The king offered a fine reward to anyone who could find out where the princesses went dancing every night. If anyone did, he could choose whichever princess he liked to be his wife and become king in time, when the present king died. Each person who tried had three nights to solve the mystery but, if he failed, he would lose his life.

The prize was so great that many sons of kings came to try their luck but, alas, no one came near to discovering the princesses' secret. Then there came to town a poor soldier who had been wounded in the war and was no longer fit for service.

He decided to try his luck at the palace and see if he could solve the mystery. On his way, he met an old woman who gave him a piece of advice: "Don't drink the wine that they will bring you at bedtime," she said. "And take this cloak. If you have the chance to follow the princesses, this will make you invisible."

The soldier thanked her heartily and walked on to the palace. That night, he was housed in a chamber adjoining the princesses' bedroom. The oldest princess brought him good food, better than he had tasted for months, and a decanter of wine. He ate a hearty dinner but he only pretended to drink the wine.

Then the soldier lay down on his bed and pretended to be fast asleep, snoring loudly.

The oldest princess looked at the soldier. "Here's another one who might have saved his life," she said.

Then she and her eleven sisters opened cupboards and drawers and arrayed themselves in their finest dresses. They were very happy, all except for the youngest, who said, "I don't know why it is, but I feel very strange, as if something bad were going to happen."

"Don't be such a goose!" said her oldest sister. "Just look

at that soldier. I hardly had any need to give him a sleeping-draught—he would probably have snored his head off anyway!"

Then she went over to her bed and tapped it, and it sank into the floor, leaving an opening to a staircase. The soldier watched all this through half-closed eyes and, as soon as he saw the princesses descending the stairs, he jumped up and threw the

cloak of invisibility
around him and followed them down.

As he hurried after them, he trod on the hem of the youngest princess's dress.

"Who's there?" she cried. "Someone trod on my dress!"

"Nonsense," said her sisters. "There's no one there. You must have caught it on a nail."

When they had all descended the stairs, they came out

into an avenue lined with trees whose leaves were made of
pure silver. The soldier broke off a twig and hid
it in his jacket. But it made such a crack
that the youngest princess was startled
and cried out, "What's that?"

"It must be a gun fired off in joy, because
we have got rid of our 'prince' so easily," said the oldest,
laughing.

They then travelled along an avenue
whose trees were made of gold and a
third whose leaves were all of diamonds,
and the soldier broke off two more twigs
to keep as evidence. Each time the
youngest princess started, but the others
took no notice.

They came to a great lake, where
twelve boats were waiting, each with
a prince sitting in it. And each princess
climbed into a boat with a prince. The
soldier slipped into the boat with the
youngest princess.

"It's strange, but the boat feels heavier than usual," said
her prince, straining at the oars.

At the far side of the lake was a castle all lit up with lanterns, and there was merry music coming from it. The soldier watched unseen as the princesses danced, each with her own handsome prince, till three o'clock in the morning.

Then the princes rowed them back across the lake and they walked wearily along the glittering avenues to the secret staircase. The soldier ran ahead of them in his magic cloak, so that he could dive back into bed, throw off the cloak and start snoring.

The princesses climbed back into their bedroom yawning and, when they were all back, the oldest tapped her bed and the staircase disappeared without trace. They undressed, discarding their worn-out shoes under their beds, as they did every night, and slept in late the next morning.

The next two nights were exactly the same. The soldier pretended to sleep, but in fact followed the princesses and their dancing-partners to the castle on the underground lake. And on the third night, he took a wine-goblet from the castle and hid it in his jacket.

After the third night, the soldier was summoned before the king. The king asked his usual question, but with no great hope:

"Where do my daughters dance their shoes to pieces every night?"

And the soldier replied, "In an underground castle with twelve princes," and he showed the king the three twigs of silver, gold and diamonds, and the wine-goblet from the castle.

Then the princesses knew that their secret was out and their dancing days over. The king told the soldier to choose which princess he would have for his wife.

"I am no longer a young man," said the soldier, "so I will take the oldest."

They were married that same day and the soldier was promised that he would be king himself, in time. But as for the twelve princes, they never saw their dancing-partners again.

Fee, Fi, *Fo, Fum*

Quick Wits
and Giantkilling

Puss in Boots

Once upon a time there was a poor miller who had three sons. When the old man died, he left his sons three things: his mill; his donkey and his cat. Well, the oldest son took the mill, of course, and the second son took the donkey, so the youngest son had to be content with the cat.

The cat was no ordinary one, however, and promised that he would help his new young master to gain a fortune.

"Just get me a pouch to wear round my neck and a

pair of leather boots, and you will see what will happen," said the cat.

So the young miller's son had a pair of leather boots made to fit his cat and a pouch for him to wear round his neck. The cat had a plan, you see, and he put it to work straightaway. He filled the pouch with lettuce and then he went and lay down outside a rabbit-hole and pretended to be dead.

The cat hadn't been lying there for long, all stretched out and with his eyes closed, when a foolish young rabbit smelled the lettuce and crawled into the pouch to get it. Immediately, the cat sprang to life and killed the rabbit. But, instead of bringing it home for his master's supper, he took it to the palace of the king.

"A present from the Marquis of Carabas," he said, standing on his hind legs and laying the rabbit in front of the throne.

"The Marquis of Carabas?" said the king. "I've never heard of him, but I thank him for his kindness."

A week later, the cat put seed in his pouch and caught a pair of plump partridges, using the same trick. He took them to the king, too.

"The Marquis of Carabas presents his compliments," he said to the king, "and offers you this brace of partridges from his estate."

"How kind of the Marquis!" said the king. "Please thank your master for his present."

And so it went on for several months. Every week the clever Puss in Boots would take His Majesty something that he had caught and pretend it was from the Marquis of Carabas.

One day, while he was at the palace, the cat heard that the king was going to take his daughter for a drive by the river. Now this princess was the most beautiful young woman that Puss in Boots had ever seen, and he had been waiting for this moment.

He rushed home and told his master to do as he said and he would win a fortune.

"You must go down to the river tomorrow morning and bathe naked in the water till the king's carriage comes by. Leave all the talking to me."

So, the next day, the miller's son went down to the river and took off his threadbare clothes, which the cat hid under a rock. Then, as soon as he heard the carriage wheels coming, the cat started crying and wringing his paws.

"Help! Help!" he cried. "The Marquis of Carabas is drowning!"

Now, the king recognised the cat who had been bringing him presents for months, saw the young man in the water and ordered his driver to stop.

"Oh, thank you," said Puss in Boots. "Thieves attacked my master and stripped him of his fine clothes. Then they threw him in the river!"

By now, the princess was looking out of the carriage window as well, and saw the miller's son splashing about in the water. She thought he was the best-looking young man she had ever seen.

"Oh, quick, Father, the marquis is drowning! Whatever shall we do?"

The king ordered his footmen to pull the young man out of the water and made one of them give his coat to him. Then he sent another to fetch the finest suit of clothes from the palace—and a towel.

When the young man was dry and dressed, he looked quite handsome enough to be a marquis. The princess smiled at him and the king invited him to join them on their drive.

Puss in Boots ran ahead and

came to a field that was being
harvested. He said to the men
working in the field, "When
the king asks you whose
field this is, you must
say it belongs to the
Marquis of Carabas,
or you will be
chopped into
tiny pieces!"

The cat was so fierce that the workers believed him
and, when the king's carriage came by and the king asked,
"Whose field is this?" they replied, "It belongs to the
Marquis of Carabas, Your Majesty."

"A fine crop you have there," said the king to the
miller's son.

"Yes," said the young man. "That field always does
well."

Puss in Boots ran ahead again and came to an orchard
full of fruit trees. He said to the fruit-pickers, "When the
king asks you whose orchard this is, you must say it
belongs to the Marquis of Carabas, or you will be chopped
into tiny pieces!"

The fruit-pickers were terrified and so, when the king drove by and called out, "Whose orchard is this?" they replied, "It belongs to the Marquis of Carabas, Your Majesty."

The king congratulated the miller's son on his fine harvest of apples and plums, and so it went on. Every field or orchard or fine piece of land they passed seemed to belong to the young marquis and the king was more and more impressed. So was the princess, for she was already in love with the young man's handsome face and she didn't mind at all that he also seemed to be very rich.

Running on ahead, the hard-working cat came to a

castle which belonged to an ogre. He sent in a message that he wished to pay his respects, and the ogre agreed to let him in.

"I have heard," said Puss in Boots, "that you are able to turn yourself into a really large animal, like an elephant. I don't mean to be rude, but I really find it hard to believe."

"Then I'll show you," said the ogre, and he took a deep breath and turned himself into a monstrous lion.

Puss in Boots was terrified and leapt onto the roof,

which was very difficult in boots. He only got down when the ogre returned to his usual shape.

"That was remarkable!" said Puss in Boots. "Now, tell me, can you also make yourself small? For that might be even more difficult."

"Not at all," said the ogre, and straightaway turned himself into a tiny mouse scampering across the floor.

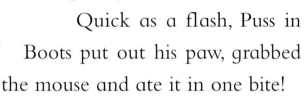

Quick as a flash, Puss in Boots put out his paw, grabbed the mouse and ate it in one bite!

When the king's carriage drew up outside the ogre's castle, there was Puss in Boots at the gate, bowing and greeting the party.

"Welcome to the humble home of my master, the Marquis of Carabas!"

And the miller's son handed the princess down from the carriage and escorted her into the castle, just as if he had lived in it all his life.

There was a fine banquet laid in the dining-hall, because the ogre had been expecting friends to lunch. The miller's son invited the king and princess to join him at the table. And all the ogre's servants were so scared of

Puss in Boots that they didn't say a word. While the king was drinking his wine and eating his cold chicken, he saw how the young people were looking at one another. "How would you like to be my son-in-law, Marquis?" he said.

"Very much indeed," said the young man, smiling, and he was married to the princess the very same day.

Now the clever Puss in Boots lives in luxury and never has to catch mice at all—but he does it sometimes anyway, just for the fun of it.

Jack and
the Beanstalk

There was once a widow who had one son, called
Jack. He was the apple of her eye but he was an idle,
thoughtless fellow. He spent his mother's money carelessly
so that, in time, it ran out and they had nothing left but
their one cow.

"It's no good, Jack," said his mother. "We will have to
sell the cow if we are to have anything to eat. You must
drive her to market and be sure to get a good price for her."

"All right, Mother," said Jack. "You can trust me."

And he set off to market with the cow. But, on his way, he met a man who had some curious coloured beans in his hat. The man saw that they had attracted Jack's attention and asked him where he was going with his cow.

"Why, to market," said Jack. "I am going to sell her."

"Well, why don't you save yourself a journey and sell her to me for these five beans," said the man. "They're magic beans, you know."

Jack thought that his mother would be glad to see him back so soon and the cow sold so easily, so the foolish boy exchanged the good milking cow for a handful of beans.

And was his mother pleased? She was not. In fact, for the first time in his life she flew into a temper with Jack and boxed his ears!

"Stupid boy!" she scolded. "Now what are we to live on? Magic beans, indeed—let's see if they fill your belly tonight!"

And she threw the beans out of the window. Jack went to bed supperless and very miserable; he was not used to being in his mother's bad books.

Next morning, when he looked out of the window, he couldn't believe his eyes.

A huge beanstalk had grown up, higher than the house. In fact, it was so high, no one could see the top of it. In spite of his mother's fears and warnings, Jack decided he would climb it and see what was at the top.

So he climbed and climbed, until he was sure he must reach the sky. After some hours, he arrived at the top and found himself in a strange country. It was very desolate, with nothing but rocks and boulders around.

Jack could see a big house in the distance and he set off towards it. It loomed bigger and bigger as he got near it, for it was, in fact, a giant's house. Jack clambered up the huge steps to the door. The giant wasn't at home, but his wife answered Jack's knock at the door. He asked her for food and drink but she told him to go away.

"You will be in great danger when my husband comes back," she said.

"He eats human beings and he'd make short work of you."

But Jack begged and pleaded and, in the end, she let him in and gave him something to eat, and then hid him inside the stove. Just in time, for the giant was coming back and Jack could hear his mighty footsteps rumbling up the stairs.

When the giant came into the kitchen, he looked round suspiciously, sniffing the air, and said,

"Fee, Fi, Fo, Fum,
I smell the blood of a human one!"

But his wife persuaded him that it was just his supper chops he could smell. (Wasn't it lucky that she was frying them on top of the stove and not roasting them inside it?) Jack was quivering with fear in his hiding place.

The giant ate thirty-six huge chops for supper and twenty pounds of potatoes. Jack thought he would never stop. Then the giant called for his wife to bring him his pet hen. Jack couldn't believe how gentle and kind the horrible giant was to the little hen. But then she laid an egg— of pure gold! Now Jack could see why the giant was so fond of her.

It wasn't long before the giant was asleep and snoring. Jack crept out of the stove, snatched up the hen and ran out of the giant's house. He didn't stop running till he reached the top of the beanstalk and climbed awkwardly down it, with the hen under his arm.

His mother was waiting anxiously for him at the bottom of the beanstalk.

"See, Mother," said Jack. "I am not good for nothing. I have brought you a hen to replace the cow."

"Well," said his mother, "it will be good to have eggs to eat even if we have no milk to drink."

"These eggs are not for eating," said Jack, and he set the little hen gently down on the ground, where she laid an egg of solid gold.

Jack and his mother lived very well after that, selling the golden eggs. Their larder was always full and they bought themselves another cow and some ordinary hens.

But Jack could never forget his adventure up the

beanstalk, of which he had said little to his mother, as she tended to worry about him. As the months went by, he felt more and more restless and eventually he just had to go back up it again.

His mother tried to stop him, but it was no good. He disguised himself, in case the giant's wife should recognise him, and set off on his long climb.

The country was just as before and he made his way back to the giant's house and knocked at the door. The giant's wife didn't recognise him but she refused to let him in.

"Not long ago I took pity on a poor lad like you and he stole my husband's magic hen," said the giantess, "and now I never hear the end of it."

But Jack flattered and cajoled her and, in the end, she let him in and fed him and hid him in a cupboard. Not much later, Jack heard the sounds of the giant returning.

"Fee, Fi, Fo, Fum,

I smell the blood of a human one,"

said the giant, sniffing the air.

"Nay, it is nothing but the side of beef I am roasting for your supper," said the giantess.

Jack watched through a crack in the cupboard door while the giant ate the whole side of beef and three apple pies, each the size of a dustbin lid. All the time he was eating, the giant was grumbling to his wife about the loss of his hen.

After his supper, the giant called for something to amuse him and his wife brought him his sacks of money to count, which was a favourite hobby of the giant's. Jack's eyes nearly popped out of his head when he saw how many silver pieces spilled out of one sack. And then the gold coins which poured from the other! Jack

had never seen so much money. He waited till the giant was asleep and snoring again. Then he crept out of the cupboard, snatched up the sacks and staggered to the door. He was terrified that the giant would wake up, but he was too full of food. So Jack made it safely to the beanstalk and carried down the sacks of treasure.

How pleased his mother was to see him safe! And she was amazed by the silver and gold. For three years, she and Jack lived happily and prosperously. Their house now had every comfort; they ate well and slept on soft beds. They had the garden enlarged, to include an orchard and a vegetable patch.

But it was still dominated by that huge beanstalk and, in the end, Jack just had to climb it again. His mother was against it and pleaded with him not to go. But the spirit of adventure was strong in Jack.

Besides, he had grown a lot in three years and he now had a beard, so he didn't think the giantess would know him.

He climbed the beanstalk again and went to the giant's house a third time. The giantess didn't want to let him in.

"It has always ended badly for us whenever I have let a human in," she said.

But Jack was a charmer and used to getting his own way. In the end, she let him in and fed him and then hid him in the copper. Shortly afterwards, Jack heard the giant coming home.

"Fee, Fi, Fo, Fum,
I smell the blood of a human one!"

he bellowed as he came into the kitchen, his nose twitching.

"It is only the pig I am roasting for your supper," said his wife. But the giant was still suspicious and hunted round the kitchen. Jack sat shivering in the copper, sure he would be caught.

At last the giant sat down to his supper and ate a whole pig, and a cauldronful of jelly and custard. He drank a whole barrel of wine to go with it. Then he called for his wife to bring him his harp.

Now this was a magic harp which played the most wonderful tunes all by itself. Jack was enchanted by the sound of it and determined to steal this, too. He waited till the giant was asleep and snoring, then crept out of the copper and snatched up the harp.

But the harp, being magic, called out, "Master, Master!" and the giant woke up! Jack tried to run, but he was so scared he was frozen to the spot. Then he saw that the giant was too full to chase him properly. This gave Jack back his courage and he started to run.

The giant ran after him and, if he had eaten less, he would easily have overtaken him. As it was, he followed Jack to the beanstalk and started to climb down after him. Jack scrambled down as fast as he could, still clutching the harp.

He reached the ground and dashed to the garden shed for an

axe, as the beanstalk was shaking with the weight of the giant. Jack hacked at the tough beanstalk with his axe and it began to creak and sway. Then it fell to the earth, bringing the giant down with a dreadful crash. He lay stretched out dead, taking up the whole of the vegetable patch.

Jack's mother was as glad to see the end of the beanstalk as Jack was to know the giant was dead. They lived happily in the same house for years and never lacked for food again. And Jack settled down and became just the sort of son his mother had always wanted.

The Three Billy Goats Gruff

Once upon a time there were three goat brothers who lived in a field together. They spent their days munching the long green grass and then skipping and playing around in their field.

But one day, they noticed that the grass in the field didn't look so green any more.

"Look," said Great Big Billy Goat Gruff. "We've eaten all the best grass. It seems much greener in that field there over the wooden bridge."

"That's right," said his brother, Middle Billy Goat Gruff. "That grass is much lusher and juicier than ours."

"So why don't we go there?" said their baby brother, Little Billy Goat Gruff.

"Mmm," said Great Big Billy Goat Gruff. "It's not as simple as that. You see, there's a bad old troll living under that bridge. He tries to eat everyone who crosses over."

"Then we must think of a plan," said Little Billy Goat Gruff.

Next morning, the bad old troll was sleeping under his bridge, when he heard the sound of hooves trit-trotting across the wooden planks.

"Goodie," he thought. "Here comes breakfast. I haven't

had anything to eat for days."

And he started to sing a horrid little song:

> "I'm a troll,
>> fol-de-rol,
>
> I'm a troll,
>> fol-de-rol,
>
> I'm a troll,
>> fol-de-rol—
>
> And I'll eat you for my breakfast!"

And he leapt out from under the bridge to pounce on Little Billy Goat Gruff who was trit-trotting over the wooden bridge.

Little Billy Goat Gruff's heart was pounding, but he bravely stood his ground.

"Please, Mr Troll," he said, "I don't think that's a good idea. You see, I'm only a little kid and I wouldn't make much of a meal for you. In fact, I wouldn't be more than a mouthful. Why don't you wait for my big brother? He'll be along in a minute and he's much bigger than me."

The hairy troll scratched his head.

"Well, all right. If you're sure he's coming soon."

And he let the little kid trot on over the bridge and into the new field.

The troll spent a very hungry morning until he heard the sound of some more hooves clip-clopping over the wooden bridge.

"Aha!" thought the troll. "That little kid was telling the truth. My tummy will soon be full."

And he started to sing his song again:

> "I'm a troll,
> fol-de-rol,
> I'm a troll,
> fol-de-rol,
> I'm a troll,
> fol-de-rol—
> And I'll eat you for my dinner!"

Out jumped the troll and there was Middle Billy Goat Gruff halfway across the bridge. He looked much meatier than his little brother.

"Oh, Mr Troll," said Middle Billy Goat Gruff. "You don't really want to eat me. I'd

only make a snack for a large troll like you.
Why don't you wait for my big brother, who
will be coming along soon?"

The troll was really hungry now, but
he was also very greedy and he liked the
idea of eating an even bigger goat. So he
let the middle brother go clopping on his way
across the bridge and into the other field.

All afternoon the troll listened out for
the sound of his goat meal trying to cross
the bridge but all he could hear was the
rumbling of his own tummy. And then, at last, when the sun
was going down, the bridge started to tremble and the sound
of hooves came stomp-stamping over the wooden bridge.

Aha! thought the troll and out he leapt, singing:

> "I'm a troll,
> fol-de-rol,
> I'm a troll,
> fol-de-rol,
> I'm a troll,
> fol-de-rol—
> And I'll eat you for my supper!"

When he saw Great Big Billy Goat Gruff, the troll's mouth began to water. The other goats had been right: there was plenty of eating on their big brother. But what was this?

The big goat wasn't frightened by the troll and his song. Great Big Billy Goat Gruff lowered his big head, with its big horns, and charged. He butted the troll high up into the sky . . .

Over the fields . . .

Over the hills . . .

. . . and right over the sun, till he was quite out of sight. And the bad old troll was never seen again.

Then Great Big Billy Goat Gruff stomp-stamped on his way, over the wooden bridge, and joined his brothers in the field where the grass was green as green. And for all we know, they are living there still.

Clever Gretel

Gretel was a cook and a very good cook, too. Her pastry was light as a feather, her gravy was rich and thick as treacle and her puddings smelled good enough to tempt an emperor away from his banquet.

But she wasn't over-particular about taking what didn't belong to her. So Gretel would swig down her master's wine and eat up her master's best meat, saying, "Well, the cook must taste the food and drink, or how can she tell if everything's all right? I have my reputation to think of."

She was also rather vain and she wore shoes with red

heels and dresses with big skirts that swirled when she walked. "You're still a fine-looking woman, Gretel," she would say to herself.

One day, Gretel's master asked her to prepare two plump chickens for dinner, as he had invited a friend to join him. So Gretel plucked the chickens and stuffed them with onions and herbs and breadcrumbs and rubbed them with butter and salt and turned them carefully on the kitchen spit, making sure they were equally cooked on all sides.

When they were nearly ready—tender and tasty on the inside, brown and crackling on the outside—she called up to her master, "Is your friend here yet? If he doesn't come soon the chickens will spoil."

"I'll go and remind him, Gretel," said her master, and he took his hat and set out.

Gretel removed the spit from the fire and wiped her face; it was hot work turning the spit for hours.

"I think I'll just go down to the cellar and quench my thirst," thought Gretel.

So she went down the stairs into the cool cellar and

took a long drink of her master's wine. "My, my, that was good," she said, wiping her mouth. "I think I'll finish the bottle. He'll never notice." So she did. Then Gretel went back upstairs, a little unsteadily, and thought she had better put the chickens back over the fire, so that they were hot when the two men arrived. But after a while, she convinced herself that one of the wings on one bird was burning. Gretel went to look out of the door to see if her master and his friend were coming, but there was no sign of them.

"It would be a shame to waste that wing," she thought, so she pulled it off the chicken and nibbled on it till it was all gone. Gretel hiccupped.

"That bird looks a bit lop-sided with only one wing. I'd better eat the other one," she said. So she did. "Where *are* those two men?" she fretted. "All my good cooking is going to be spoiled."

She hated to think of it going to waste so, in the

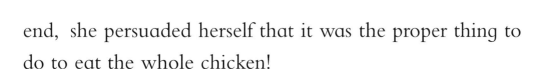

end, she persuaded herself that it was the proper thing to do to eat the whole chicken!

"That was delicious," said Gretel. "I really am a very good cook." Then, after a while, "I don't think Master and his friend are ever coming. The best thing to do with that other chicken is to send it the way of the first." So she ate the second chicken, too.

When she had finished and thrown all the bones into her stockpot, Gretel heard her master opening the door.

"My friend is coming right behind me," he said. "I'll just sharpen the carving knife. I'm really looking forward to those chickens!"

And he went into the dining-room and started to sharpen his carving knife on his steel. There was a knock on the door, but he didn't hear it. Quickly, Gretel ran to answer it. And there was her master's friend on the doorstep.

"Oh, please don't come in!" she whispered. "My master means to cut off your ears, not sit down to dinner with you. Can't you hear him sharpening the knife?"

The poor man looked scared out of his life and immediately ran home as fast as he could.

"Has my friend come, Gretel?" called her master.

"Oh, what a villain!" cried Gretel. "He ran into the kitchen, snatched both chickens and ran off with them!"

"What?" cried her master. "Both chickens? He might have left me one. I'm very hungry."

And he set off after his friend, waving the carving knife and yelling, "Just one! Just one!"

But the friend, thinking he meant "just one ear" didn't stop until he reached his own house and got inside and bolted the door. I don't suppose the two men had anything more than bread and cheese for their supper.

But Gretel went to bed with a very full and satisfied tummy. "I am a very good cook," she yawned, before falling fast asleep.

Brave Molly Whuppie

There was once a poor couple who had too many children. So they took the youngest three, who were girls, and abandoned them in a wood. That was a terrible thing to happen but the youngest girl, Molly Whuppie, was very brave and clever and she kept her sisters' spirits up.

They all walked through the wood until they saw a light shining and came to a big house. When Molly knocked at the door, a woman came but, when Molly said they were three hungry girls, she shook her head.

"I dare not help you, my dears. My husband is a giant

and who knows what he'll do if he finds you here when he gets home?"

But the three girls were too tired to go any further and sank down on the doorstep in an exhausted heap. So the giant's wife took them in after all and gave them some warm milk in front of the fire.

They were just beginning to feel better when they heard the giant coming home.

"What's this, Wife?" he shouted. "You know better than to allow humans in my house!" And he would have hurt the girls, but his wife stood in front of them and said, "Leave them alone. They're doing you no harm. Go and eat your supper."

The three girls stayed the night and they had to sleep in the same bed as the giant's three daughters. Clever Molly Whuppie noticed that the giant put gold chains round his daughters' necks but gave Molly and her sisters straw necklaces to wear. Molly stayed awake and, when all the other girls were asleep, she swapped the gold necklaces for the straw ones.

The giant came in and felt for the necklaces in the dark. When he had found what he thought were the strangers, he started hitting them with a stick. But it was his own daughters and they set up such a screeching that the three other girls were able to escape during the commotion.

They ran and ran till they came to the king's palace. There Molly Whuppie told him the whole story and threw herself and her sisters on his mercy.

"Amazing!" said the king. "You've done very well and got those valuable gold chains. But you would have done even better if you had got the giant's sword that he keeps behind his bed. If you can fetch that back for me, I'll marry your eldest sister to my eldest son."

So brave Molly Whuppie went back to the giant's house all by herself and crept into his bedroom while he was sleeping. Quietly, she reached for the giant's sword, but

it clanged against the iron bedstead and woke him up.

He jumped out of bed with a roar, chased Molly out of his

house and ran after her till she reached the Bridge of One Hair. (It was called that because it was so narrow.) Molly danced over the bridge waving the sword, but the giant didn't dare set foot on the flimsy bridge. So he just shouted:

"Woe betide you, Molly Whuppie,
If you ever come again!"

But Molly just laughed and sang back:

"Twice again you'll see me, giant.
All your ranting is in vain."

She ran back to the palace with the sword, and the

king was so pleased that he married Molly's big sister to his oldest son that very night.

"Now," said the king, "if you were able to bring me the purse that the giant keeps under his pillow, your other sister could marry my second son."

Molly had been expecting something like this, as she knew that the king had two more sons, so she set off again for the giant's house. As before, she crept into his bedroom, but it was much more dangerous this time, as she had to slip her hand under his pillow. Just as she was doing this, a strand of her hair fell over the giant's face and he woke with a huge sneeze.

Again he chased her all the way to the Bridge of One Hair, but he couldn't catch her.

"Woe betide you, Molly Whuppie,
If you ever come again!"

he bellowed.

"Once again you'll see me giant,
All your ranting is in vain,"

sang back Molly Whuppie, and ran back to the palace with the giant's purse. The king married Molly's other sister to his second son that very night.

"You know I have one more son," the king said to Molly Whuppie. "And if you would bring me the ring from off the giant's finger, you could have the youngest prince for your own husband."

Molly had been expecting something like this, so she set off back to the giant's house. This was going to be the most dangerous adventure of all.

For the third time, she crept into the giant's bedroom. He was snoring loudly. Molly gently tugged the ring on his finger, but it wouldn't move. So she pulled as hard as she could. The ring came off—but the giant woke up!

He grabbed Molly in his big hand and she couldn't get free, however much she wriggled. "Aha!" he cried. "I've got you now! Tell me what you would do if I had done as much harm to you as you have to me."

Quick as a flash, Molly Whuppie said, "I'd put you in a sack with a pair of shears and a needle and thread and hang you up in the hall. And then I'd go into the wood and choose the biggest stick I could find and bang the sack with it till you were black and blue."

"Right," said the giant. "Then that's exactly what I'll do to you!"

And he took Molly and stuffed her in a sack with the shears and the needle and thread and hung her on the wall and then he went off into the wood to look for a really big stick. Meanwhile, Molly said, "Oh, if only you could see what I see!"

The giant's wife was interested in spite of herself. "What do you see?" she asked. But Molly just kept saying, "Oh, if only you could see what I see!" until the woman begged her to let her into the sack.

So Molly cut a hole in the sack and jumped out and let the giant's wife take her place. She sewed up the hole in the sack with the needle and thread. Just then, the giant got back with his big stick and started to hit the bag. But his wife screamed out and he realised that clever Molly had tricked him again.

Molly ran out of the house and reached the Bridge of One Hair at top speed. The giant lumbered up behind her, panting,

"Woe betide you, Molly Whuppie,
If you ever come again."

"Never more you'll see me giant,
I shall never come again,"

sang Molly, and she ran back across the bridge to the palace. As soon as she showed the king the giant's ring, he arranged for her to marry his youngest son. So there

was a splendid triple wedding of the three sisters to their three princes, who all lived happily ever after. And Molly never did see the giant again.